H. R. F. Keating was the crime books reviewer for *The Times* for fifteen years. He has served as Chairman of the Crime Writers Association and the Society of Authors, and in 1987 was elected President of the Detection Club.

He has written numerous novels as well as non-fiction, but is most famous for the Inspector Ghote series, the first of which was made into a film by Merchant Ivory and won a CWA Gold Dagger Award.

In 1996 H. R. F. Keating was awarded the CWA Cartier Diamond Dagger for outstanding services to crime literature. He is married to the actress Sheila Mitchell and lives in London.

BREAKING AND ENTERING

All Bombay is buzzing with news of the murder of millionaire Anil Ajmani, who was found stabbed to death in his heavily guarded mansion. Every inspector in the Crime Branch hopes to be the one to nail the killer — and that includes Inspector Ganesh Ghote. Unfortunately, he has been given the less glorious task of tracking down the cat burglar, nicknamed Yeshwant. Aided, or perhaps hampered, by his old friend Axel Svensson, Ghote fights to uncover Yeshwant's true identity — and finds that he may be the one to solve the murder of Anil Ajmani after all . . .

Books by H. R. F. Keating
Published by The House of Ulverscroft:

EDITED BY:
THE MAN WHO . . .

A REMARKABLE CASE OF BURGLARY

AN INSPECTOR GHOTE MYSTERY:
BRIBERY, CORRUPTION, ALSO

H. R. F. KEATING

BREAKING AND ENTERING

An Inspector Ghote Mystery

Complete and Unabridged

ULVERSCROFT
Leicester

First published in Great Britain in 2000 by
Macmillan Publishers Limited
London

First Large Print Edition
published 2002
by arrangement with
Macmillan Publishers Limited
London

British Library CIP Data

Keating, H. R. F. (Henry Reymond Fitzwalter), *1926 –*
Breaking and entering.—Large print ed.—
Ulverscroft large print series: mystery
1. Ghote, Ganesh (Fictitious character)—Fiction
2. Police—India—Bombay—Fiction
3. Bombay (India)—Fiction 4. Detective and mystery
stories 5. Large type books
I. Title
823.9'14 [F]

ISBN 0–7089–4639–9

Published by
F. A. Thorpe (Publishing)
Anstey, Leicestershire

Set by Words & Graphics Ltd.
Anstey, Leicestershire
Printed and bound in Great Britain by
T. J. International Ltd., Padstow, Cornwall

This book is printed on acid-free paper

1

Despite everything, Inspector Ghote found his head filled with pleasantly vague thoughts. Yes, the month of October was not the best time to be footing it here and there about the city. It was almost as hot as full summer, plus the last of the monsoon showers made it sweatily humid. And, yes again, the case he had been given was not very likely to bring him success.

It would have shown more of respect for my abilities, he thought, if instead of this fag-end affair I had been sent, like every other inspector in Crime Branch, to work on the Ajmani murder. To be the one who put the handcuffs on the fellow who in that altogether mysterious manner succeeded to get right inside that double-and-triple protected house . . . Altogether feathers in my cap.

But what has been given to me? When you are coming down to it no more than a fellow climbing in to commit a handful of B and E offences, breaking and entering under Indian Penal Code Section 446, *Whoever commits 'house-breaking' after sunset and before sunrise is said to commit 'house-breaking by night'*. Very well. Serious enough crimes. But not at all so serious as murder, the crime that nothing can put back.

But Deputy Commissioner Kabir has put this case into my hands now and no one else's. My responsibility.

He felt it as a heavy weight thrust on to him. And all, he thought, because Pinky Dinkarrao in her *Pinky Thinking* column that everyone is reading was comparing the climbing thief I am expected to find to Yeshwant, the big ghorpad lizard that in times past carried a rope up rocky crags to capture impregnable forts. And from then on the sunset-to-sunrise fellow was grabbing all the headlines. Until the Ajmani murder put every other thing into shade.

Still, there is one good side to it all. I am on my own. No one here to tell me to do things the way they want them done. True, not much of excitement just only going round where other officers have already been, trying to pin down this fellow, month after month defeating best efforts of local stations. Even now of Crime Branch itself. But in the end there may be something of kudos for whoever is nabbing this Yeshwant. And perhaps it may be myself. Even if so far I have not hit on one new fact. Modus operandi same each time: in through a high window, and out with one

2

first-class haul. And never a single physical clue.

And there is another reason, in the humidity and the heat, to be glad I am neither sitting under the fan in my flat nor within reach of my wife at the end of a telephone. Things at home are not at all peaceful. Trouble is Ved. A young man of his age, even if he is still a student, should be out on his own. But how can anyone, unless they are fully rich, find money for even the smallest of rooms in a city that is boasting its top rents are higher even than those in great Manhattan? So there the boy is, wanting to live his own life, and bumping up at every moment against his mother, living her own life.

There had been that ridiculous business last night. Ved using the TV to play some video he had bought from a pavement vendor, some damn nonsense of *Lost in Space,* and it coming up to time for *Swabhimaan,* Protima's favourite programme. Ved, when she had pointed this out to him a few minutes beforehand, muttering a promise to let her switch over, but then sitting on, glued to those Western imported spacecraft adventures of some Americans called the Robinson family. And, when Protima had reached across and switched over herself, he had shouted, *Be for once getting out of my hairs*.

And he himself had walked right into it all. There was Protima using her tongue, which he occasionally thought of, in secret, as 'sharp as a fish knife' with in his mind's eye a fishwalli from Sassoon Docks or Mahim Bay gutting pomfret after pomfret with single strokes of her razor-keen blade. And there was Ved blustering almost as loudly. *Does she think she is owning me still? I am no more her little baby*. And Protima retorting with quieter but more stinging words.

No, better by far to be tramping the fiercely hot streets, going from one rich robbed lady to another, only to be told time and again that they had already answered each and every police question.

He found himself now at the end of the long stretch of the Oval Maidan. Almost without realizing it he came to a halt in the shade of the thick trunk of one of the tall Royal palms fringing the long spread of still-green post-monsoon grass. Half a dozen cricket matches were in progress. He stopped for a moment to watch, switching between games played so close one to another that an alert boy in the outfield of one could catch an overambitious batsman in another, or even in two others.

Or he saw, as he felt the hot throbbing wall

of held-up early rush-hour traffic almost singeing his back, there was one fielder at least taking no part in either of the games to each side of him. He was a boy of ten or eleven, plainly lost deep in some private dream, eyes raised to the horizon, totally motionless.

Suddenly Ghote remembered an occasion when he himself, at much the same age, had been taking part in an untypically dull game, almost British in the way the batsmen had been cautiously poking at each delivery. Relegated to the deep field, he had fallen into a similar faraway reverie, idly holding out in front of himself the ancient sola topee his mother insisted on him wearing. And then, with a heavy little thump, the ball had landed exactly in that basin-like hat. He had come to, blinking, to shouts of laughter from every other fielder, the two batsmen, even the boy umpiring, and, mortified beyond anything, had run from the scene.

So what he had never been able to ask afterwards was whether that ball had landed in his old topee as the result of a batsman's stroke — and would that have given him a catch? — or whether some fellow fielder, seeing him in his lost-to-the-world daze, had crept up and tossed the ball in. It was something that, from time to time, he still wondered about.

Behind him, he became aware, breaking into his present reverie, of a loud tapping noise, almost a hammering.

He turned.

A huge tourist coach, *Rajah Super Airbus* in florid letters of gold all along its red and cream painted side, had been held up in the inching-forward, fumes-belching traffic. Inside it, he could just make out through its heavily tinted glass someone banging on a window with the heel of his hand while at the same time agitating the other arm as violently as if he were a captive being led away to death.

He looked round. There was no one else near him.

Can the fellow be signalling to myself only?

He wondered whether to turn and walk away. What could anyone in a tourist bus, probably full of white firinghis, want with him?

And, besides, he felt furious at the way his pleasant cocoon of thoughts had been broken into.

But then he saw that the figure behind the tinted window — and, yes, he was wearing a foreigner's white suit — was blundering along towards the front of the vehicle. A moment later its door slid open and its steel steps descended.

'It is Mr Ghote? Inspector Ghote?' a tremendously loud voice boomed out into the vibrant heat of the day.

But who . . . ? Who in this huge tourist bus is knowing my name? And why? Why are they calling and calling at me?

He shook his head in bewilderment.

This big firinghi in the white suit, with his red-red face and — I am seeing just only now — those blue-blue eyes —

But —

But it is. It must be . . . It is Mr Svensson. Mr Svensson from Sweden, who was here making some UNESCO report years and years ago, soon after I was joining Crime Branch and was investigating that Perfect murder. That poor old Parsi, Mr Perfect, who in the end was being not so perfectly murdered but recovering under the first rain of the monsoons and living also some years more.

Mr Svensson here now.

So I must . . .

He went up to the shiny steps of the bus and reached forward, hand held out.

'Mr Svensson, it is you? Here in India? But what for have you come? You are making a new UNESCO report, yes?'

7

'But it is Axel, my friend. You always called me Axel. And I called you Gandhi. You remember?'

'Well, it is Ganesh.'

'Yes, yes. Ganesh. Ganesh Ghote, my old friend.'

But now the storm of violently irritated hooting from the whole stream of vehicles held up behind the huge tourist bus at last impinged on the Swede.

'But — But we must not keep all these good people waiting behind. Come in. Step up. Ride with me. We are coming from the airport to the Taj Mahal Hotel. Would going there be too far for you? Otherwise we may never meet anywhere else.'

Ghote calculated quickly.

He had been making his way, unhurriedly, to the Bombay Hospital in Maharishi Karve Road, which he still sometimes thought of as Queen's Road as it had been when he first came to Bombay. One of Climbing Yeshwant's victims was now a patient there and he had hoped to discover when he would be able to see her. But that could wait. He was hardly likely to learn anything that would enable him to arrest the miscreant before the day was done.

'Very well, Svensson sahib.'

'But it is Axel. Axel, er, Ganesh. You must

8

always call me Axel.'

The cacophony of hooting had grown even louder.

'Come in, come in.'

The big Swede seized Ghote's hand, dragged him up and in. The door swished closed behind him.

He felt at once an extraordinary coolness. The huge coach, he realized, was fully air-conditioned. No wonder Axel Svensson had been able to wave and shout so energetically. Without shedding one drop of sweat.

Stumbling along to the seat next to the one the Swede had occupied he felt as if he had been miraculously removed to another world. And it was quiet. The hooting of the vehicles behind could no longer be clearly made out. The roar and clatter of the huge city all around seemed to have been cut off with the sharp efficiency of a heavy steel shutter descending. There was space to breathe.

But hardly space to think. Axel Svensson was torrenting out questions.

'So, Ganesh, what is it you are doing these days? You are still in the police? Have you risen above the rank of inspector? You are in command somewhere? Or are you still in —What was it called? Yes, the Crime Bureau.'

'The Crime Branch. Officially even it is the Detection of Crime Branch of the Mumbai Police.'

'Mumbai Police? Mumbai? But this is Bombay. I booked to go to Bombay.'

'Yes, yes. This is Bombay. But these days it is being renamed Mumbai, the name they say it was having many, many years ago. So now I am finding myself a member of the Mumbai Police — '

But the big Swede broke in.

'My dear Ganesh, I have to tell you some sad news. My wife, my dear wife of twenty years, is dead. A sudden illness. And I am left a widower. But your wife? I remember her so well. Parvati.'

'Protima.'

'Yes. Yes. And she is well. And children? You had a little son. Are there more now? Sons? Daughters?'

'No, we were never having more of children.'

'Well, my beloved Gosta and I did not have children. That is why when she was dying I felt so lost. I had nobody. Only my older brother, the very opposite to me in temperament, looks, height, everything. As short, you may say, as a dwarf. In the end I decided I must get right away from Sweden. And I remembered my time in India, so

10

different from Sweden, so much sunshine and light, so much life. And how I had shared your investigation of the Perfect murder. I thought how much I would like to meet you again. And now, what a fine chance. Here you are, when I have not been one hour in Bombay. No, let me get it right. In Mummai.'

'No, no, you should say Mumbai. Mumbai. And, look, Mr Sven — Axel, look. We are almost at the Taj.'

'The Taj Mahal Hotel? Yes. Yes, I remember it from all those years ago. A fine building. And I had a magnificently comfortable stay.'

'So, now I am knowing where you are, it would be very, very easy to ring you up and perhaps arrange to meet again.'

'But, no. No, my dear Ganesh. I have a lot more to hear about your life nowadays. A lot more. We have scarcely begun. So you must come inside. It will not take much time, I think, to complete the formalities. And then you must have a good long drink, and tell me all about yourself and your family and your work. You are on some Number One priority case, ja? Something like the Perfect murder, eh?'

Ghote felt the questions and the demands entering his head like so many busy invading

11

rats. With difficulty he contrived to answer the last one.

'Number One priority, no. No, that is the Ajmani mystery. No, I have another case. Not altogether like the Perfect murder. But I will explain.'

2

Waiting with some impatience to sort out this newly arrived complication in his life, Ghote sat looking through the huge windows of the Taj's Sea Lounge at the solemn arch of the Gateway of India, at dirty whitish launches chug-chugging off to take tourists to the wonders of Elephanta Island, at the repeated explosions of flocks of grey-winged pigeons disturbed at their feeding, at a passing vendor of long multi-coloured ribbons streaming brightly out from his high-held stick. At anything.

The process of showing Axel Svensson to his room seemed to be taking a good deal longer than he had expected. No doubt dealing with a large party of foreigners would produce problems. Some might speak rather poor English. More might understand India's English with difficulty. But he wished it was not taking quite as long as it was. Voices in the big hotel were too brayingly intrusive for him to be able, in the words his schoolmaster father had quoted so often, to *retreat to his Northern fastness*, his happy state of cut-offness before that booming *It is Mr*

13

Ghote? Inspector Ghote? had broken in on his cricket reverie.

A large upright woman wearing a richly coloured, heavily gold-bordered sari, a great roll of fat at the small of her back, was standing directing a large party to sit where she felt proper. 'Mohan will go there. Brij must be here. Radha there . . . ' Then a spoilt child in a blue cotton two-piece, labelled *Boston Red Sox*, was staggering unchecked between the tables, the piled-high ice cream in his hand spilling blobs of sticky rose-red all over the floor. A party of young men and women were recklessly ordering Black Forest pastries and, the Sea Lounge speciality, Hearty Sandwiches.

Just the sort of young students, Ghote thought with a jab of bitterness, whose parents have flats big enough for them to be out of the way all the time. Far, far beyond what I am able to have.

Up on the dais at the far end, a suited, tie-wearing piano player tinkled out an unending stream of notes, passing seamlessly from one half-recognized Western song to another. Well, Ghote acknowledged, at least here is someone who has managed to find a world of his own.

Then at last Axel Svensson came blundering in and loudly hailed him.

'There you are, Ganesh, my friend.'

Ghote forced himself not to wince. But he hardly liked to think that he was being pointed out by name to everyone in the big room. If he saw more of his former friend, was his quiet going to be broken into like this time and time again?

He agreed, when the big Swede, seating himself, had noisily called out, rather too many times, 'Waiter! Waiter!' to drink a beer. Waiting for the order to come, he took a good look at his acquaintance of old. The years had altered Axel Svensson. He was still as tall and as broad as before, a looming presence, even if now a little stooped. But his once strikingly fair hair was a soft grey, and his face, which had been, as he remembered, bonily athletic, was altogether heavier, even ponderous. If it was ever a matter of full-out running, as it had been chasing a suspect during the Perfect case all those years ago, he would not last very long.

Mercifully, there was no possibility of that sort of collaboration now.

'So,' Axel Svensson came boring in, 'tell me just what it is you are doing. Tell me it all.'

'Yes.' He gathered himself up. 'Yes. Well, I am, as you guessed, still at Crime Branch. And still in inspector rank only.'

'Ah, but soon you will be getting a

promotion, yes? Perhaps from the case you are working at this very day. I am willing to bet on that.'

Ghote wished he would not.

'Then I am afraid you would be losing your money. No, I know now that I shall end my career as just only inspector, and I am not at all minding. And certainly there is not likely to be very much of kudos for me in the case I am on.'

'But how is that? Why isn't it some top-priority affair? Like that — What was it you were mentioning? Some mysterious business? A name like Amjani? Why aren't you on the Amjani case?'

'It is Ajmani. Ajmani. Not Amjani. Mr Ajmani is — or he was — the head of Ajmani Air-Conditioning, one of the most important concerns in India.'

'And he has been murdered?'

'Yes. So you see, even if the circumstances were not highly mysterious, as a person of very, very much influence the case would be having the full attention of Crime Branch. Then also he has a past which was not very much of above board.'

'Aha. Now, what was this past?'

Ghote would have preferred not to go into details. All right, Anil Ajmani was known to have achieved his great wealth by doubtful means. But nevertheless spelling out those means to a foreigner, a firinghi, was something he hardly wanted to do. But the question had been put, with all the force of a bulldozer advancing into a slum under demolition.

'Oh, nowadays all that is well brushed away,' he answered. 'But in the Bombay of old it was not easy to get to the top in industry unless you already had much wealth, or unless you were prepared to pay some altogether unscrupulous people to do dirty works for you. People like the ones everybody is nowadays calling the bhai log. The how would you say, the Brother People.'

'I see, something like the Mafia. And your Mr Ajmani used such people to build up this air-conditioner empire of his?'

'Oh yes. It must be all in the files somewhere. If same has not kindly been misfiled after a good bribe has been paid. There would be some strike-breakings. Perhaps even one or two quiet killings of people in the way. By hired goondas. Not able to be traced. A matter of what is called paying for supari. You are knowing those little digestive chips of betelnut we like to eat after a meal? They are supari. And to pay for supari is to pay to have some awkward morsel digested.'

'So not a very nice individual, your Mr Ajmani.'

'No, not at all nice. Out at Madh Island two-three years back he was building himself a big new house, and he was calling same Shanti Niwas, that is House of Peace. That was because he had thought it necessary to build one very high wall round it and to install also each and every latest security arrangements. People said he was altogether wise, even now when he is a highly respected man, to have done so much.'

'And his death, you were saying, was in some way mysterious?'

'Yes. For the one and only simple reason that he was murdered in the very middle of that house of his. Despite his each and every precaution. No one should have been able even to penetrate inside that high wall. But so far no one has been able to see how it was done. But there, in the heart of his place of safety, in a room he was calling as his den, a room where no one was admitted without first knocking, not even his wife, Ajmani sahib was killed. Stabbed to death. A single blow.'

'Yes, it would seem to be most mysterious. But why are you not the investigator, or, if the case is demanding the complete attention of your Crime Branch, why are you not on the team out there at Muddy Island? Why is that?'

Another boring-in demand.

'Well, Mr Sven — No, Axel. No, first of all it is Madh Island. We are spelling it in English M-A-D-H. It is a place towards the Greater Mumbai Municipal Limit. Not strictly nowadays an island, though once it was. Now more some sort of peninsula. But very tranquil. Very quiet. Very much of country-side. With sea also.'

'But you are not there, investigating? That seems to me a damn shame.'

The fellow never able to be diverted?

Ghote sighed.

'Perhaps,' he said, 'Deputy Commissioner Kabir, who is now heading Crime Branch, may not share the good opinion you have of myself. So what has happened is that I have been ordered to take up the inquiry which before the Ajmani murder was more or less a priority for Crime Branch.'

'So, what is that? It was what you were investigating when, looking out of that bus, I suddenly saw you?'

The fellow was going to find out, to the last comma. No way to avoid it.

Another sigh.

'It is like this. For many months past there has been a series of altogether daring jewel thefts in the city, each with the same MO. You are knowing *MO?*'

'Yes, yes. Latin, modus operandi. You forget until I retired I was in the Swedish Department of Justice. I know about police work.'

'Very good. Well, this badmash's MO was always to get into the apartments he was raiding by climbing up to some open window. It was not mattering to him whether it was just only four-five floors high or twenty. So after a while the papers began calling him as Yeshwant.'

'Yeshwant? Who is Yeshwant?'

'I will tell. I am supposing you do not know anything about our great Mahratta leader, Shivaji Maharaj. Shivaji fought many, many successful wars in years 1640 to 1680. That is his statue with sword upraised down there beside the Gateway. Perhaps you remember seeing it from your first visit?'

'I don't think so. But I will take good care tomorrow to go and inspect this Mr Shivsati.'

'It is Shivaji. Shivaji.'

Ghote could not keep the sharpness out of his voice.

'Yes, yes. Shivaji. I will remember.'

At least fellow is sounding somewhat of rebuked.

'Well, it was Shivaji's habit to take with his

20

army a ghorpad, what they are calling in English a monitor lizard. You know such creatures are very, very good climbers. On more than one occasion Shivaji was able to capture a high-up fort by tying a rope to his pet ghorpad, which he was naming as aforesaid Yeshwant.'

'A very nice story. I like it very well.'

'But not such a nice story for us in the police. Every child in Maharashtra has heard it, and with each and every paper taking it up this modern-day Yeshwant was becoming one popular hero. So Commissioner sahib was ordering full-out Crime Branch investigation. Every inspector, except only myself, stuck at Headquarters on paperwork bandobast duties, was investigating. Some of the previous inquiries may not have been one hundred per cent thorough, you know. However, nothing new was found out. But then came the Ajmani murder, and all Crime Branch inspectors were put on to that, except I myself was given the Yeshwant case.'

'Yes. I see that doing work that has already been done by others, going round in the hope you may pick up some scraps that have been neglected, is hardly going to get you promotion.'

'Well, I am no more looking for that. But I would have very much liked to be out there at

Shanti Niwas, with my share of Ajmani investigation. However, as I am not, I am content to be looking into Yeshwant's activities in peace on my own.'

'Yes, yes. I understand that. It is a great thing to be one's own man. But tell me, have you yourself found any clue, even one, leading to this daring fellow?'

'No. I must answer no. In the two days I have been on the case I have visited, let me see, twelve, no, it is thirteen, of Yeshwant's victims. In all it must be some two-thirds of them. And it could have been almost the same story at each place. Yeshwant was climbing up to a window left for some reason open. He was getting inside in the darkest hour of the night. He was seizing only one piece of most valuable jewellery, such as something from that very, very famous shop in Zaveri Bazaar, Pappubhai Chimanlal. And he was climbing down again, not seen by anybody.'

'But fingerprints? Was he leaving his fingerprints there? I believe the fingerprints of a monitor lizard would be very easy to see.'

Axel Svensson gave a donkey bray of laughter. Heads turned. Ghote wished he could, like Sita in the *Ramayana*, be swallowed up in the earth.

'No, no,' he said. 'The officers who had

22

investigated before myself, even the fellows from the local police stations, had of course looked for fingerprints. When victims of a crime are people of wealth full procedures must be employed. But they were never finding prints that could be identified in police files.'

'But footprints? Did you observe any footprints those officers had missed? A burglar climbing in like that must have left footprints.'

'And in rich homes there are servants who, first thing, are sweeping all the floors. And in a rich home also no memsahib is going to be up very, very early in the morning starting to raise hell when she is discovering that the fine piece of jewellery she had just bought at Chimanlal's was no longer where she had left it after some big party the night before.'

'Yes. Yes, I suppose you are right.'

Ghote tried to suppress the twinge of pleasure he felt at having checked so decisively at least one thrust of his foreign friend's inwards-borings.

'There was even a time reported to the police,' he said, 'when Yeshwant went away empty-handed because the lady had had the good sense to lock away her new diamond necklace. She was only realizing a burglar had been there when she was finding a window in the high-up flat, which she had left just one inch open, was now open wide.'

'But I suppose Yeshwant took something else. Some small and valuable antique he happened to see?'

'No, he was taking nothing whatsoever. It seems this ghorpad will eat just only the finest jewels.'

'Very good, very good.'

The big Swede launched into another boisterous laugh, thumping the table flat-handed until their beer mugs jumped.

Ghote regretted making his attempt at a joke.

'You know,' Axel Svensson said when at last his laughter had subsided, 'I am beginning to be most interested in this daring Yeshwant of yours. Most interested indeed.'

'Well, I suppose he is one criminal who is giving out more of interest than most. Yes, he is very, very daring. And also — What shall I say? — yes, quality-minded. Deputy Commissioner Kabir, who is very much a reader of English literature, when he was giving me my orders was calling him as a Raffles. You are knowing Raffles?'

'Yes, yes. Your Mr Kabir is quite right. Raffles, the gentleman cracksman. As a boy I read those stories in translation. Raffles would steal only the rarest objects, and from

24

the most rich. A discriminating criminal.'

'So I am all the more wondering, if in the end we are nabbing this what you are calling discriminating criminal, what like he will turn out to be.'

'And so am I wondering. So am I.'

The Swede finished his beer with one lengthy swallow. He looked across the little round table at Ghote.

'Ganesh,' he said, on a suddenly lower, even plaintive, note. 'Ganesh, my friend. Do you think . . . ? Do you think that, possibly, possibly, I could accompany you in your investigation? The way we were doing when it was the case of the Perfect murder. We were good collaborators then, yes? I was even of some help to you. Wasn't I?'

Ghote realized now that all along he had half-feared such a request being made. But what he had not at all expected was the sad tone of supplication. He guessed what lay behind it. Axel Svensson, back in Sweden, had suddenly found himself a lonely man. His wife dead before her time. No children. Nobody, except a brother, he had said, different from himself in every way, as sometimes brothers could be.

So an appeal was being made. A cry from a distance. The Swede wanted more than the brightness and cheerful noise of his remembered Bombay. Something to seize his interest, take him right away from unending gloomy thoughts.

But that he could not, he must not, provide.

'Mr Svensson,' he said. 'Axel. You must be knowing that it is impossible to allow a civilian, and a foreigner even, to take part in an official police investigation. Would this happen in Sweden? In UK? In America?'

'No. No, I realize I have been asking too much. Only . . .'

It was that infinitely human *Only* that finally did it.

'Nevertheless,' Ghote heard himself say, 'perhaps because of the help you were able to give me all those years ago, I will stretch one point. Yes, Axel, from time to time you may come with me as I am making my inquiries.'

3

Ghote had told Axel Svensson before he had left him that his *from time to time* proviso would mean he could not be accompanied to the Bombay Hospital to see the patient he had hoped to interview there when that roar of *It is Mr Ghote?* had burst in on him. He had, in fact, some hopes of learning from this Parsi lady, Mrs Marzban, something that might get him nearer daring and discriminating Yeshwant. The officer who had interviewed her earlier was likely to have learnt little from someone soon to be admitted to hospital. Perhaps, now that she was under good care, he would have better luck.

But when he rang from home, after ascertaining that no new Yeshwant burglary had taken place overnight, he was told Mrs Marzban was in fact already on her way to the operating theatre.

A check. But there was the next address in his notebook, an apartment in one of the toweringly tall blocks up on Malabar Hill called Landsend. And, since he had told Axel Svensson he would not call for him until midday, he thought, without much violence to his conscience, he could go to this substitute interview on his own. Not having a huge hovering foreigner at his elbow to be somehow explained away was altogether too tempting, whatever twinge of regret he felt about not taking the sad man out of his gloom.

However, he set off on his motor-scooter hardly feeling ready to tackle the possibly difficult task ahead. His head was filled by a dull resentment. He knew he had in fact little to complain about. His breakfast puris had been as crisply puffed-up as Protima always made them. Some remnants of her quarrel with Ved over *Swabhimaan* and *Lost in Space* had been rumbling on, but those he could have dismissed as the sound of distant thunder. The trouble was the way he had been woken from his comforting end-of-night dozing dream.

What had brought him back to the world was an unexpected caress from his wife. He did not usually resent such advances, and he had very soon responded. But all the same his happy state of half-awake dreaminess had been broken into. It had not been the time that such things should take place. His response, he acknowledged now, had lacked enthusiasm. Which must have been why those puris, however crisp, had not gone down as well as they usually did, and why he felt more than a little unfitted for the tactful interview he suspected lay ahead.

But soon he found he was becoming cushioned from all that the outside world could throw at him by the pleasant vibration rising upwards from his feet, planked down on his machine's ridged base. Despite the city's as ever wildly erratic traffic all around him, he began at last to feel ready to tackle Mrs Latika Patel, wife of a Member of the Maharashtra Legislative Assembly, a man who was, more to the point, son of a prominent minister. Care would be needed, and he felt now he was comfortable enough within himself to give it.

There was little about the actual break-in, some weeks earlier, to take into account. It had been one of Yeshwant's most audacious, and most successful. He had climbed the huge towering block, as usual in the darkest period of the night. He had eased back the flat's open kitchen window, had evidently waited patiently till the cook, who had recollected being a little disturbed as she slept on the floor there, had gone back to sleep. And then he had silently crossed the narrow little room and entered the master bedroom. There, he had not at all interrupted the

29

deeper slumbers of heavily pregnant Mrs Patel and her spouse and had simply picked up off the dressing table Mrs Patel's latest acquisition.

It was perhaps the richest haul he had yet had. According to the full description supplied by Pappubhai Chimanlal and Co., it was a necklace in the form of tiny linked gold monkeys from which hung in a diamond-studded setting an immense cushion-cut Sri Lankan sapphire. Mrs Patel, it appeared, had taken advantage of the last wedding she was likely to attend before she gave birth to display it. But, tired out that evening, she had failed to put her expensive acquisition into the safe behind the painting of a stallion, groomed and adorned for a procession, hanging opposite the marital bed. But the real mystery was how Yeshwant had got to know that the loot was there to be taken. If Mrs Patel, tactfully handled, could give a clue to that, an arrest would be that much nearer.

The happy sphere of quiet Ghote had eventually grown round himself as he rode up Malabar Hill and along Dongersey Road was abruptly shattered, however, when he reached the tall block. A band of sex-changed hijras, engrainedly mannish despite the gaudy saris they flaunted, must have learnt that there had been a birth in one of the apartments in the building and had come to demand the tribute customarily given when a new human being came into the world.

Mrs Patel, he thought with a tumble of dismay. Hadn't she been about to have her baby? Or was it that she had already done so? Plainly, if she was being invaded now by this rabble of men-women, she would be in no mood to answer detailed questions. And invaded she would be. Eunuchs always claimed that when in far-off times Lord Rama, exiled to the forest, had ordered back 'the men and the women' who had wanted to follow him he failed to address those who were neither men nor women. So they had shared, at a distance, the god's fourteen-year exile, and thus had gained special privileges. One of which was that of bestowing a blessing on a newborn child, and getting a reward for it.

Why, oh why, did obstacles like this spring up whenever there seemed to be a hope of making progress? But nothing for it now but to wait and see if Mrs Patel really was the hijras' target.

They appeared to have arrived not much before himself, and seemed to have only just begun dancing and singing to the lively beat of the tabla which one of them was playing, long flexible fingers swiftly moving on the little drum's twin surfaces. Their aim at present was partly to attract passers-by and partly to induce the new mother — would it be Mrs Patel, or not? — to come out to receive eventually the blessing *May the little one live long.* And their leader, he noticed now, was really a beautiful creature. He was wearing a sari as boldly striking as those of his companions but, a pure lemon yellow, much more attractive. He even looked not unlike oval-faced Shabana Azmi, the film star. His eyes made to appear enormous by a skilful application of black kohl. A flashing red nose-jewel setting off the purity of his skin. Long silver earrings drawing attention to two neat, close-to-the-head ears. Vivid red outlining elegantly shaped lips.

Ghote felt a tremor of disturbance. The hijras' dancing presence was forcibly upsetting all his customary feelings about the opposite sex.

He debated for a moment whether he should leave at once. He could come back at a better time.

But, no. He would not be made to run away by such a coarse band invading not only the home of this new mother but, worse, the quietude of his own mind.

He was glad, a few minutes later, that he had stood his ground. The new mother came out at last into the building's forecourt, carrying her baby. Her young husband, looking a little sheepish, accompanied her. And it was clear they had come from one of the ground-floor apartments. So not Mrs Latika Patel.

Ghote knew he ought now to enter the building, find a lift, go up to the eighteenth floor and its double apartment, *18 C/D*. But he allowed himself to stay where he was for a little longer, still half in thrall to this invasion of his mind by the hijra in the lemon-yellow sari.

Now that the mother of the newborn child had arrived, the next stage of the ceremony began. Swiftly under the lemon sari the dancing hijra had stuffed a bundle of clothes, and in an instant, no bad actor, he had become a heavily pregnant woman. 'May my little one have a rich family,' he sang repetitively in a voice that, deep though it was, was by no means harsh. Next he added a note of comic vulgarity, first hugging his enormous belly with 'The British gave it to me,' then repeatedly singing variations on 'I lost my nose-ring under his bed' and 'He has stung me like a scorpion.' Then, lapsing into his pregnancy role, he went on to 'Oh, I am wanting something sour' and 'Oh, I am wanting sweet things.'

At last he collapsed into the lap of one of his fellow men-women, one dressed in a vilely vivid wide green skirt with a choli in shiny black and silver stripes above it. There he went through the motions of giving birth, with many a groan and moan of pain. Until at last he rose, the bundle under his sari adroitly transformed into a hardly visible baby in his arms. He went across to where, in the surrounding semicircle of applauding onlookers, the new mother sat, half-smiling. Cunningly loosing the clothes bundle, he appeared to bestow on the real mother the real baby already in her lap.

A hand to bless her. An embrace for the uneasily grinning new father, not without its share of sexuality. Hastily from his shirt pocket the father took the stapled wad of small denomination notes he had put there in advance. And the invasion was over.

Quickly Ghote slipped past the still-delighted crowd, ran up the steps of the building, found the liftman he had hoped for, shot upwards.

He found Mrs Latika Patel, when a servant had ushered him in, sitting plumply comfortably in one of the huge brocaded armchairs in the big, coolly air-conditioned drawing room, its tables laden with pieces of fashionable tribal art, its walls dotted with gold-framed mirrors, its floor richly silk-carpeted. She had a baby in her arms — to judge by the tiny pink dress, several weeks old — and was looking still almost as much a new mother as her neighbour down in the forecourt.

'Madam,' he began sharply, when he realized he was getting little of Mrs Patel's attention. 'Madam, I very much regret it has become necessary to ask further questions about the theft from this apartment one month past. Police has, I am sorry to tell, failed so far to obtain any information leading to the arrest of this criminal they are calling by the name of Yeshwant.'

Mrs Patel at last glanced up from cooing at her little daughter.

'Yes,' she said. 'A terrible, terrible shame.'

Ghote felt a little disconcerted. But he rallied to the defence of Crime Branch.

'Shame, yes,' he said. 'But kindly remember that an investigation of this sort is not at all an easy matter. When the thefts — '

'No, no. The shame of it is my losing my sapphire. Already my guru is telling me I should be wearing some new one, or my ill-luck under Saturn will go on and on. But how can I be finding time to go to Pappubhai Chimanlal and Co. when I must be nursing my little Amrita? But then Guruji is saying this is not yet the time when I can finally emerge from the cloud Saturn has shadowed me with. My seven years of bad fortune are not quite over yet.'

Ghote had no particular belief in astrological predictions. But he felt he should at least keep the baby-struck mother talking.

'Seven years?' he said. 'So what it was, madam, that caused you to come under such a curse?'

'Who shall say, Inspector? Who shall say? Perhaps it was just that I was conceived on a moonless night. But I have at last conceived a child of my own, and under a full moon. So we may yet live a happy life.'

'Madam, I am hoping so,' Ghote brought himself to say. 'I am seeing your problem. Nevertheless, it is a vital matter for us in the police to obtain even the smallest indication concerning the identity of said Yeshwant.'

But Mrs Patel, back again to smiling down at her baby and crooning away, had plainly re-entered the cosy world she had been inhabiting when he had come in. He waited for a long minute, and then tried again.

'Madam, can you recall any circumstance of the robbery that was seeming peculiar when you were discovering same?'

No response.

'Madam? Madam?'

'Yes, Inspector? Something you were asking?'

'Yes, madam, yes. I was asking were any of circumstances peculiar?'

He thought, once more, that she was not going to reply. But after a lengthy pause she did manage to raise her head from contemplating the baby.

'Peculiar? Well, you see, when I was married . . . It was a semi-arranged marriage, you understand, and — And for various reasons it had to take place at short notice, my husband's relations going back to Europe, America, a question of the auspicious date. Many reasons.'

She dipped her head back down to her baby. Ghote thought he had lost her again. But she looked up almost at once and went on.

'So there was no time for obtaining all the jewelleries there should have been. But, when at last after six years I became pregnant, of course the first thing was to buy some good pieces in case my baby was a girl and would need a proper dowry. After so many years childless, now I am having my sweet little girl I must buy many more jewelleries. When it is coming to her wedding I must have as many jewels to give in dowry as her status is requiring.'

Now at last I have got her attention, Ghote thought, and what is she telling? Some nonsenses only about buying more and more jewellery. These rich women. Not that she is worse than most of Yeshwant's victims I have already interviewed. Almost without exception they seemed to regard police inquiries as one irritating nuisance. With each day that has passed since they have been robbed the sting of it appears to have lessened. Insurance was there, they seemed to be feeling. Why am I, they say, to be wasting my time answering each and every question this policewalla is liking to put?

And Mrs Patel was prattling on.

'We were very lucky before my sweet Amrita was born that Pappubhai Chimanlal and Co. had just made a necklace that would fit well with the very good sapphire they had. They are saying they will be able to make another just like it now, but only if we are giving them time to find a sapphire equally as good.'

And, with that, the excessively devoted mother turned back to her little Amrita. Eyes for nothing else.

Inwardly cursing her, Ghote found himself wondering how it was that, married for six years, the Patels had only just achieved parenthood. Some women's problem? Or, perhaps, the *semi-arranged* marriage, a negotiation where the girl could say, *No*, had been instead a fully arranged one, a contract between two families that left no room for the bride's rejection? In such cases it was sometimes long before successful sexual adjustment was arrived at, so it was no great surprise that the little girl was getting so much attention. It was good, in fact, to see a wealthy mother not passing a baby over to an ayah at the first possible opportunity.

But this was no time for such speculation. If only just one of his questions would get a proper answer. And then, too, he would like to be given permission to examine the kitchen where climbing Yeshwant had entered, and he would like to see the master bedroom and the exact place that Mrs Patel's sapphire necklace had been left.

And, most of all, he wanted to question the servants. Could any one of them have told Yeshwant that the necklace was there to be stolen?

He ought, too, perhaps, to be getting more exact details of where else in the apartment Yeshwant must have been. Somewhere still there might be some tiny piece of evidence the dizzying climber had left behind, a fragment of cloth, a fingerprint that could be identified. But what hope was there with this utterly faraway mother in front of him? The two days of his investigation had been —

His train of thought was suddenly and brutally interrupted.

The door behind him was flung open and, turning, he saw come striding in a man, wearing smart sports clothes, short of stature but nevertheless totally commanding, full-faced, double-chinned, the whole suffused with rage. He could be none other than Shri R. K. Patel, son of a minister and himself an MLA.

And it was immediately evident, as scrambling to his feet he assessed the situation, that he was not going to be able to get from the newcomer even as much as he had so far extracted from his wife. Such overwhelming rage could not be penetrated.

'Tea,' the MLA spluttered out, hardly, it seemed, taking in the fact that he was not alone with his wife. 'Tea. Where is my tea? I am coming back from Bombay Gym, tired and exhausted after my hard work-out, and where is my tea? Where? Where?'

Absorbed as she had been in her tiny daughter, Mrs Patel could not but respond to the irruption.

'Oh,' she said. 'Oh, you are back itself already? What time it is?'

'What time? What time? It is time for my

tea. And where is it? Where?'

'Oh, I had not realized it was so late. I was — Darling, this is a police inspect — Oh, please, please, Inspector, ring that call-bell that is just beside yourself.'

Ghote, a little bewildered, looked round, saw on the wall near him a big brass push-bell, pressed it.

And found that R. K. Patel's rage had, momentarily, been redirected. To himself.

'Police. Police. What in God's name is a policeman doing here? In my drawing room. Some jack-in-office itself?'

Ghote glanced back at Mrs Patel, but saw at once that she was not going to offer any explanation.

'Sir,' he said. 'Sir, I am Inspector Ghote. From Crime Branch. I am here, sir, in connection with the burglary that was taking place. Sir, one sapphire necklace, with gold chain of altogether little monk — '

'Damn it, Inspector, do you think I don't know what my own wife's stolen necklace was made of. It cost enough, let me tell you. It cost — '

But at this moment through the door that R. K. Patel had left swinging open there appeared a servant boy. Pale with terror, he was holding in front of himself a large tray on which there rested teapot, cup and saucer, sugar bowl, and plate heaped with spicy-smelling snacks. He scuttled forward and placed it all on a table beside what was evidently the master's chair.

'At last. Tea.'

R. K. Patel slumped down in the chair, reached forward, snatched the carefully folded napkin matching the tray's pretty embroidered cloth, spread it over his fat little tummy, seized a samosa from the heaped pile, thrust it towards his mouth, bit half of it off, masticated noisily.

Ghote wondered if he could after all go back to putting his questions to Mrs Patel. She had, at least, been thoroughly roused from her baby-oriented dream-world by this invasion.

Hastily he reviewed the conversation he had so far had with her. Yes, permission to speak with the servants. That must be next.

He took a short step forwards.

But from beside him, from the master chair, there came then a scream of fury, louder even than anything that had gone before.

'Teaspoon. Teaspoon. No damn teaspoon. Put sugar in my tea, and nothing to stir it with. Damn it, damn it, damn it.'

And R. K. Patel rose to his feet like a giant sea-serpent shooting up from the depths, seized the tray beside him, lifted it into the air and brought it crashing down, sending tea from the pot streaking out along the richly carpeted floor and the remaining samosas scattering everywhere like so many pieces of an exploding bomb.

Ghote saw that now the only thing he could do was to leave. As unostentatiously as he could.

But, almost at the door of the apartment and its waiting servant, he had a piece of luck. From somewhere a little further along the wide carpeted corridor there emerged a man who could only be the family guru Mrs Patel had spoken of. He was an odd-looking figure, at least in contrast to the opulent apartment he seemed to be at home in. Out in the streets half a dozen wandering sadhus, three white stripes across their foreheads, might look much as he did. But here he stood out. He was, to begin with, totally naked except for a cloth hanging from his somewhat fleshy hips and twisted under his loins. Then his hair, which was grey almost to whiteness, had been allowed to grow to its fullest extent and appeared to be caught up behind him in half a dozen loose ropes, coloured by the years to an unappetizing yellow.

But, despite his outward appearance, he at once betrayed, in speaking in excellent

English, a degree of education no one would necessarily have expected.

'Good morning. I believe I am addressing Inspector Ghote?'

'Yes. Yes. But how were you knowing . . . ?'

A roguish twinkle in the old man's eyes.

'Are you looking for supernatural powers, Inspector? Have you forgotten that servants talk?'

'Oh, yes. Yes. Yes, I suppose that is the answer.'

He wished once again that he had been able to question these servants. Was it possible that one of them might have sent a message somehow to Yeshwant telling him that the necklace was there for the taking?

'Yes,' the curiously disconcerting guru went on. 'That has given you one answer. And I am able to set your mind at rest on another matter, too.'

'Yes, Guruji?'

What other matter could the man have in mind?

A smile on the full, fattish face in front of him.

'You have been hoping one of the servants here has been able to tell this famous thief Yeshwant where he could find madam's sapphire necklace, yes?'

'But — But — '

'But how did I know that, Inspector? How did I know what it was you were thinking? My mysterious powers? No, not at all. Think. Think, as I have done. What else but that would a visiting police officer want to know?'

'Well, yes ... Yes, I see now that is — Obvious.'

'Just because a man has undergone what is necessary to free himself from the world and its cares, it does not mean that he has lost all the brains God has given him, you know.'

'No, no ... I — I am sorry to — '

'But not to mind. What you are wanting to know is whether your Yeshwant had a spy in this household, yes? And I can answer that easily. How could he? How could any servant know that madam would leave her necklace outside her safe that night? And if any one of them did by some unlikely chance, how could they then tell this climbing thief of yours in time for him to come when he did? Yes, Inspector?'

Ghote thought. But he needed to think only for a moment.

'Yes, Guruji, you are right. I do not think it is at all worth surmising on the servants here any more. Thank you.'

Another faint, there-and-gone smile of the plump face.

'So, tell me, before you sensibly left madam

after that tea-tray crashed so noisily to the floor, were you finding the other questions you came here to ask answered equally well?'

Again Ghote paused a moment to think. But no reason not to tell the simple truth.

'No, Guruji. In fact I was not gaining very much of new knowledge at all.'

'Madam much occupied with her little Amrita, yes?'

'Yes. Yes, she was.'

Then an idea came to him.

'But you, Guruji,' he said. 'Perhaps you can give me some better informations?'

'Fingerprints? Footprints? A thread caught on some protruding ledge? No, Inspector. I was not here when the robbery occurred. And even if I had been I am not someone likely to notice smudged surfaces, dirt on the floor or little pieces of cotton where they should not be. I am, after all, detached from this world.'

A sharp look from his droopily large eyes.

'I think I see you are asking yourself how it can be that someone who can speak English as it should be spoken is still one who has renounced the world. Let me rid you of that problem. You see, I came from a very well-off family, and before I was twenty years of age, while I was still at college, my father and mother had found a good match for me. She was a girl in a family whose business would fit

46

in well with that of my father. Now, at that time, I was by no means averse to the feminine. I do not want you to think I was someone like those hijras down in front of the building just now. Not at all. But I felt that a marriage simply for the sake of joining two families together, although it was to a girl who though I had never seen I might have liked, was altogether too much of an intrusion upon me. So I took the only course I saw as open. I ran away. I became a wandering sadhu, and eventually I found myself up in the Himalayas, in a cave, alone. And there for some long time, perhaps it was years, I meditated. And at last I found I had filled my head with inner peace. Then I felt able to come down to the world, to my native Bombay even. And here I have been able to give advice to people facing the problems of daily life, even if I sometimes put that advice in ways they are able to accept. And so I became the guru of a distinguished family in the city, and I go also to other houses from time to time. There, does that put your mind at rest, Inspector?'

'Yes. Yes, of course, Guruji.'

Were there other mysteries this man, who seemed to know so much about what went on in this sky-high isolated apartment, could explain?

But he was not to discover.

'However, enough of myself. Or rather enough of the man you see before you, whose life I can look at from a distance as one used to look at lives in books. No, Inspector, all I have to tell you now is that you will hardly learn more from poor Latika.'

From the abruptly distant expression on the guru's plump face Ghote saw that he was going to hear nothing else from him.

'Well, Guruji,' he murmured, 'I am glad to have met.'

He turned towards the front door where the servant was still patiently waiting.

So, one other interview, he thought, when I have learnt nothing of any actual use. But somehow I must. If I myself could only be the one to lay by the heel this Yeshwant . . .

4

Ghote had promised, against his better judgment, that he would join Axel Svensson for lunch at the Taj's daily buffet. He would have much preferred to have gone straight to the next person on his list of Yeshwant's victims. He had hoped, having seen Mrs Latika Patel, that this would be to a ninth-floor flat in a block called Green Apartments at Worli Seaface. But when he had telephoned to make sure Yeshwant's victim, a Mrs Gulabchand, would be there he had been told that she was 'out at family shack, Peace and Quiet, at Juhu Beach'. But, of course, she had a mobile phone with her.

He had called her then and arranged a meeting.

So, however much he would have preferred to be going alone on his scooter in the heat to Juhu than to be sitting in the cool of the Taj, he knew he could do nothing else. But the wave of concern he had felt when it was borne in on him that the big Swede was a wretched and lonely man had made him promise to join him. He must stick to that.

From the moment, however, that they had

each collected a plateful from the long tables and found themselves chairs, before either of them had taken so much as a mouthful, he discovered his concern was going to be ill-rewarded.

'Ganesh. Ganesh, my old friend, I must tell you something terrible.'

Ghote's spirits, fragile at best, tumbled. Why did this have to happen to him? One moment contentedly on a case that required only steady work and some decent luck. Then a shout from the door of a Rajah Super Airbus and a sharp complication entering his life. Almost at once to be followed by that lancing appeal to his sense of compassion. And now, a sudden multiplication by two, those words *something terrible.* What could it be that, within twenty-four hours of Axel Svensson's arrival in India, had been *terrible*?

'But tell me what it is,' he said resignedly. 'I am sure whatsoever has happened may be put right.'

'Ah, it is not what has happened to me. It is what might happen. Or it is like a foretaste of what may happen to me, or to anyone here in India. You know, I came here with such hopes. At home everything seemed gloomy and miserable. With us, winter is a long wearing time, at its worst almost without any daylight, and cold, bitterly cold. I thought, with all the sadness I had, I could not endure the winter that is just about to begin back there. So India seemed such a hope, such a joy for me ahead.'

'Yes, yes. A winter like that must be terrible. As terrible as our summer, when it is at last getting so hot you cannot move or even think. But what it is that has made you feel India is no longer having what you were hoping would chase out your sadness?'

'It is a thing I heard.'

'Heard? Heard only?'

'Yes. Yes, I thought, as you were not able to let me come with you this morning, I would take a stroll to see how much I could remember of Bombay. No, of Mumbai. I have got it now. Mumbai.'

'Yes, a good thing to do surely?'

'It might have been. Yes, it might have been. But I had not long left the hotel when up beside me there came a man, not very well shaved, wearing just a shirt, not too clean, some no-colour cotton trousers, and on his feet a flapping pair of rubber sandals. What is it you call them?'

'Chappals, chappals.'

'Yes, chappals. So this individual came up beside me and at once he began to talk. He had very good English, which was excellent for me. You know sometimes I am hardly able to understand the English some Indians speak. Not you, my dear fellow. Not you. But with some people I have asked questions.'

Served you right for going up to people and breaking in on them with your questions-pestions, Ghote thought. But he kept his face intent.

'He was most kind, this man. And most interesting. He saw I was a foreigner and he took it on himself to tell me all about his city.'

Yes, Ghote thought. One of the many idlers who hang about the Taj, offering their services as guides. If not worse. If not as sellers of all sorts of doubtful substances, or of rupees for dollars, with cheating also.

But again he said nothing.

'So we walked a lot in the streets, the two of us. It was hot. But it was so interesting, so full of life, that I didn't mind that at all. I saw a man sitting on the kerb having his underarms shaved. I saw a small boy earning his living by hiring out a weighing scales. I saw a man in a big orange turban — from Rajasthan, my friend said — sitting playing a sort of fiddle and singing and singing all to himself. I saw so many things, women in beautiful saris in every colour under the sun, bandsmen in uniforms even more fantastic than the ones South American generals used to have. And then my friend took me to a

52

juice bar. I don't remember just where, but it was next to somewhere called the Ever New Hairdressing Hall. I remember that. I think I shall never forget it.'

'Yes, yes. But what was happening?'

'Well, first we had some excellent cold drinks.'

Which you paid for.

'And then my friend was telling me this story, this horrible story. And all the pleasure of the day was taken from it.'

'So, what was this story?'

'Listen, this is what he told me had happened. He was swearing to me it was hundred per cent true.'

'Yes?'

'There was this man. He met up with some others and they went drinking somewhere. Just as they might have done in Sweden. And then something was put in this man's drink and after a while he fell into a deep sleep. Well, that also might have happened in Sweden. Not everybody there is a saint. But in Sweden that man would have been robbed and nothing more. Here . . . Here it was different. It was worse, worse.'

'But what it was? Axel, you must tell me.'

'It was this. In the morning when he woke up he felt the most appalling pain in his back. He lay there in agony for a long while, and then at last he dared to feel behind himself. And he found — He found a piece of cloth. A piece of cloth, thick with encrusted blood. He called for help and at last was taken to a hospital. There they told him that, while he had been drugged into unconsciousness, he had been cut open and — And one of his kidneys had been taken.'

'A kidney removed? But had he, this fellow, been carried off to one of those doctors who pay the poors to give a kidney, more or less legally, to someone who is badly needing transplant? I was having some experience of that once.'

'No, no. That perhaps is rather bad. But this was much, much more terrible. The people who did this thing were not doctors at all. They were thieves. Plain and simple thieves. I suppose they sold the kidney afterwards to some unscrupulous surgeon. But it is terrible. Ganesh, there are people in this city who will dig into your very body and steal your kidney. This is a terrible place. It is terrible, your Mumbai.'

'But, no. No, Axel, my friend. Very well, I am admitting that this account you have given shows an altogether black side. But think. Howsoever much this fellow you were talking to was swearing and swearing his story was true, it does not have to be so. A fellow like that — Tell me, were you giving him money?'

'Well, yes. Yes, of course, he was giving me so much of his time that it was only right I should give him something in exchange.'

'How much?'

'Well, I was taking a fifty-rupee note from my wallet, and he was actually seeing that I had some one-hundreds there, so . . . '

'Yes. Exactly. You see, he would be wanting to push into your mind he had done you some maha favour. So that in the end you would be happy to hand over whatsoever he was asking. He was wanting to set that there in your head.'

'No, no. What he said must be true. He was swearing it was.'

'But I am telling you it is more likely it was some made-up thing. Yes, something like it may have occurred. But, if it was less of horrible, he would not have been able to make you feel you were owing him so much because he had told you about it.'

'Well, I suppose it may be like that.'

He saw the Swede making a visible effort to accept the likelier account. But he had more than a few doubts that he would ever agree completely. His mind had been too cunningly attacked.

'Come,' he said briskly. 'Eat that good food

you have put on your plate. Eat it up, and then we will be off to find if we can, this very afternoon, one fine clue to Mr Yeshwant's whereabouts.'

So, instead of riding out to Juhu Beach, Ghote had the Taj's tall colourfully turbaned Sikh doorman summon over his booming loudspeaker the next taxi in the line waiting at a respectful distance.

For some while as their journey unwound Axel Svensson remained silent, lost in thought. Yet, glancing at him from time to time, Ghote saw those thoughts were not the sort of vaguely pleasant ones he himself had managed eventually to fill his head with while he had gone to Mrs Patel perched high in her apartment at Landsend. No doubt the firinghi was mulling over and over the blackness of life that had been thrust into him in a way he had not at all expected beneath the Indian sun.

And Axel Svensson's fear was to be reinforced before they were halfway to their destination. They were halted at a red signal near Byculla Station. Suddenly on the Swede's side of the cab there came a soft, dull tapping on the glass as insistent as the thumps Axel Svensson had delivered to the window of the Rajah Super Airbus to gain the attention of his friend of years past, rapt in that cricketing reverie.

It was, of course, a beggar tapping. But it was not with an ordinary beggar's dirt-encrusted, claw-like hand. It was the stump of the man's amputated arm that was being softly banged in a steady, demanding rhythm on the window, through which no doubt he had spotted the Swede's white face.

'Take no notice,' Ghote said quietly. 'You should not allow such a fellow as this to trouble you.'

'But no,' Axel Svensson replied. 'No, the poor man has lost his arm. No, look. Look, he has lost both arms. He must be unable to do any sort of work. I must give him something.'

He rummaged in the inside pocket of his suit for his wallet.

'Give him just only a coin, if you must give,' Ghote said. 'You know, the fellow is actually working. Begging is his work. That is part of life in Bombay that has always been here. You must accept same, and not be letting such people break in on your peaceful feelings.'

'Well, if you say so.'

But Axel Svensson, digging into his trouser pocket, produced a good handful of silvery coins, wound down the cranky window — and found it impossible to put his gift into non-existent hands.

The beggar, however, skilled in his trade, contrived quickly to swing forward the little leather bag he had tied round his neck. The coins went in. And, to Ghote's relief, the light ahead turned to green and their taxi shot away.

At least, he thought to himself, the beggar was not one of those women who go round with a dead baby, hired by the day. What would my soft-hearted friend have mistakenly done about one like her?

Happily the rest of the journey went without incident, and by the time they had passed Juhu's Sun 'n' Sand Hotel, haunt of film stars, and come in sight of the beach, with its scurrying children, its predatory fortune-tellers, its depressed-looking riding camels, its monkeywallas and acrobats, Axel Svensson was beginning to show signs of enthusiasm about the interview ahead.

'Perhaps, my friend,' he said, 'before much longer you will actually be hot on the trail of Yeshwant.'

'Perhaps.'

They had no difficulty in finding the Gulabchand shack, boldly labelled *Peace and Quiet*. Standing in the doorway of the comfortably substantial beach-side house was a person who could be none other than Mrs Gulabchand herself. Tall and imposing in a plain blue cotton printed sari, if one that was gold-bordered, she was imperiously supervising a sweeper with his stick-bundle broom swishing at the sand on the fenced-off wooden deck in front of the house.

'No, no. You have left some there. There. Yes, there. Brush it away. I must have the place clean. Brush it. Brush. Whatever dirt and filth there may be on the beach, I am not having it brought on to my property. Not by so much as one sand-grain. Sweep. Sweep.'

Ghote went over and introduced himself, adding in a slightly shame-faced patter, 'And this is Mr Svensson, from Sweden, he has written many reports for UNESCO on Indian policing methods.'

Mrs Gulabchand appeared to accept the Swede's intrusion placidly enough.

'Shall we go inside?' she said. 'I must apologize for this little place. It is not like my home itself. But I have to come out here when I can. Otherwise the pressures of my social engagements become altogether too great.'

'Madam,' Ghote said, 'I quite understand.'

His sympathy, however much contrived, earned them immediately a servant bringing tea. When they were settled with it, in a great deal more comfort than Mrs Gulabchand's apologies had warranted, Ghote gave a little cough and began.

'I am well knowing, madam, you may have been asked all this before. But I am having to admit we are becoming altogether desperate to get even one clue that would lead us to the man they have named as Yeshwant.'

'You should be desperate, Inspector,' Mrs Gulabchand proclaimed. 'That badmash was climbing right up to our apartment. On ninth floor itself. He was entering by one of the windows in — In our bedroom. Our bedroom, Inspector. How he was having the daring to do it I cannot imagine.'

'And when were you realizing that he had made away with' — Ghote consulted his notebook — 'with one pearl choker necklace, valued at two lakhs of rupees.'

'No, no, Inspector. That choker was worth much more than that. A great deal more.'

'I regret, madam. I was quoting only the description given by Pappubhai Chimanlal and Co., from whom you were purchasing same only three weeks before the theft itself.'

'Very well. Let us say two lakhs. It is not important.'

'No, madam. But I was asking when you were realizing choker was not there.'

'It was first thing in the morning, Inspector. I am always up early. I like to take

60

down a tray of food for a cow that an old woman brings to the front of the building each day. I have a nice silver tray I keep especially for the purpose. I would not like it to be used for anything else when the cow has licked it, even after thorough washing. The woman comes always at seven, so if I am to be there before other people I have to be up in time to have my bath and get decently dressed. I would like even for the woman to be earlier, but the man she rents the cow from will not give it at the right hour. You can expect no more of such people these days, Inspector, I am sure you will agree.'

'Yes, madam, yes. And that is bringing me to the question of your servants. Madam, do you believe any one of them may have somehow told this Yeshwant you had just bought your pearl choker?'

Mrs Gulabchand thought. Ghote could almost see her servants lined up in front of her as she pitilessly probed into each humbly bent head. But at last her face brightened.

'No, Inspector, no,' she said. 'I am sure that such a thing was not happening. You see, I am always altogether most careful to keep all my jewelleries in the safe. The servants would not be knowing all I have got. It would be wrong if they did so.'

'Wrong, yes, madam. But on the night that

Yeshwant climbed up to your apartment you had left your choker out of the safe, yes?'

'Yes. Yes, Inspector, I had. You see my husband had just been made president of his local Lions Club, a great honour. A great charity organization. So . . . so there had been a party. And, Inspector, when we were getting home, at two a.m. itself, I was altogether exhausted. There had been so many people to see, to talk to. And so, just that once — I promise you, just that once — I did not open up the safe.'

'I see, madam.' Ghote sighed, if hardly accepting the *just that once*. 'I suppose Yeshwant had been watching your apartment and had seen you returning so late, and then when at last the light in your bedroom was shut he was climbing up. It must have been something like that.'

'And it was wrong that it should be, Inspector. Wrong.'

'Yes, madam. But you were telling how and when you saw that choker had gone next day.'

'Yes. Yes, it was not until I had got back from feeding the cow.'

Axel Svensson, who had been showing signs of restiveness, leant forward sharply now.

'Please,' he said, 'why is it you feed a cow? And from a tray of silver? Why is that?'

62

Ghote could have kicked him. But, happily, Mrs Gulabchand seemed pleased enough to instruct a firinghi.

'The cow is sacred in India, sir,' she said. 'One gains great merit by feeding her. And all the more so if the food is properly served. In conditions of utmost cleanliness. The people you see buying bundles of dirty grass from women leading cows in the streets will not get their prayers very well answered in that way. I can assure you.'

'But does the cow — '

Ghote jumped in before more harm was done.

'Mrs Gulabchand,' he said, 'I am sorry to be questioning and questioning. But you may have noticed some small thing at the time of discovering the theft that would give us in the police just the line we are looking for. So, may I ask please, whether you were seeing anything out of place near where your choker was when this Yeshwant was lifting same?'

'You are asking if there were dirty footmarks or something, Inspector? Let me assure you that my house is always in a state of full cleanliness. Whatever may be outside my door, I can promise you that inside everything is perfect. Perfect.'

'But, madam, Yeshwant may have left his footmarks just only two-three hours before you were getting up to feed your cow. You could have seen same.'

'Impossible, Inspector. Impossible. No one would dare leave dirt on my bedroom floor.'

For a moment Ghote wondered if he could point out the illogicality of what she had said. And then he saw that Axel Svensson was about to do just that. Quickly he decided that, however little he had learnt, he was unlikely from as self-regarding a person as Mrs Gulabchand to learn more.

'Madam,' he said. 'You have been most kind. But what I now need is to inspect scene-of-crime itself. When will you be back at your so wonderful and perfect home?'

'You may come tomorrow, Inspector. Or, no, that may not be a good time to have the police coming into my apartment. So, say, next day. Or soon. Soon. Telephone me.'

5

In the taxi going back, Ghote found himself
becoming yet more irritated by Axel Svensson
than when the Swede's interruptions had put
an end for the time being to questioning Mrs
Gulabchand. The firinghi seemed to be
gripped now by the hunt for Yeshwant to the
exclusion of almost everything else. All too
plainly he was feeling, too, that the case was
not being handled in the way it would have
been in Sweden.

'But all the same,' he broke out again, 'you
could have insisted Mrs Gulab-whatever gave
you a definite appointment. She is making
you run here and there and telling you
nothing. And you could have insisted on
asking her more out there. You should
have — '

He stopped himself with a rein-jerk of
last-second politeness.

'No,' Ghote said, sharp in resentment at
this continuous breaking in on his own
thoughts. 'I am well knowing people like Mrs
Gulabchand, so rich she is not at all living in
same world as myself. Yes, if such a person
should happen to be a murder suspect or a

key witness even, then you must go on and on at them. Go on until it gets into their heads that they must think about what you are saying and give answers. But when it is a less important case, and after all this is a matter of B and E only, then it is no use to press and press. In the end it will come down to the husband complaining to State Minister for Home.'

'B and E? What's that? It's not a term we use in Sweden.'

'Oh, it is just only breaking and entering. Breaking and entering. Not at all nice for any victim, but not the most serious crime under Indian Penal Code.'

'Yes, yes. I see that. But all the same — '

'No. No, Axel sahib. No use to be talking and talking. That is all there is to be said.'

He had not meant to be that brutal. But he felt he had endured enough probing questions.

There was silence from then on. After a while Ghote did not know how to break it. He began almost to wish that, when they stopped at a red signal, another beggar would come up beside the big Swede to tap-tap-tap at the taxi's window, smeared already by dozens of demanding fingers, by as many peeringly inquisitive snot-running noses.

But no beggar appeared. So they both sat

without a word, and before long Ghote found he had succeeded in *retreating to his Northern fastness*, there to puff out a fine protective cocoon of vaguely pleasurable thought.

He had made it so prick-proof, in fact, that, although he had intended to reverse his order to the driver to go first to Police Headquarters and then to take Axel Svensson to the Taj, he forgot to do so. The taxi came to a halt inside the compound at Crawford Market before he had realized where they were.

Well, he thought, it is not any big problem. Svensson sahib can stay with me while I go to my cabin to collect any messages, and then I can send him off to the hotel and spend some time quietly writing my reports. In any case, perhaps it may please him to see once more the cabin where, all those years ago, we sat and discussed the Perfect murder. Perhaps, in spite of everything, I owe him that much.

But he was not destined to reach his cabin as quickly as he had imagined.

'Halloo, halloo,' a resonant female voice called out from behind them. 'Halloo, Inspector Ghote.'

He looked back.

It was as he had expected. From the doorway of the little Press Hut just by the nearest entrance gate to the compound there had emerged a woman of about forty, greying hair a wild tangle, face gaunt, stick-thin body carelessly wrapped in a highly coloured red and green cotton sari, a big battered old leather satchel banging against her hip.

Turning to Axel Svensson, he explained.

'It is one Miss Dinkarrao. She is a journalist. Known by the name of Pinky itself. She was the one who was first calling the climbing thief as Yeshwant.'

'Yeshwant? It was her who was telling that story of Maharajah Shivsena and his climbing lizard?'

Ghote let out a long sigh.

'Axel sahib,' he said, 'it is not Shivsena. It is Shivaji. Shivaji Maharaj. You must have seen the name Shiv Sena on some wall-writing somewhere. It is a political party. Shiv Sena is meaning the Army of Shivaji. They are very much fighting to keep our state of Maharashtra for Maharashtrians only. And when I am saying *fighting*, that is what I am meaning. They were the ones who were insisting and insisting on Bombay turning back into Mumbai, even though it was fifty years after the departure of the British who were always calling it Bombay.'

'Yes, yes,' Axel Svensson said hastily. 'But this lady, this Miss Pinky, she must be following the Yeshwant inquiry with great keenness. Will she be able to tell me more about him, what he has done in the past, what he is likely to do now? That is the thing.'

Ghote felt a new descent of depression as he realized that the Swede, if he got talking to Pinky Dinkarrao, would be all the more enthusiastic in wanting to have a full share in the hunt for Yeshwant.

'Inspector, Inspector,' the angularly thin journalist called out now. 'Just the man. I was hoping to catch you. I hear that you have been made sole in-charge of the Yeshwant case. I want to know what you have discovered. Those crime reporter fellows can think of nothing else now but the Ajmani murder, and all they have to write about it is that somehow the servants there have been eliminated. Nothing interesting in that. So I thought I should get something more into my column about just how Yeshwant is being tracked down.'

Oh no, Ghote thought, falling yet deeper into gloom. Now I am to have two questioners-pestioners riding on my head. First Axel Svensson, now Pinky Dinkarrao.

Nothing for it, however, but to speak to Pinky, whatever traps and trip-ups she may lay for me to make out hunt for Yeshwant is being disgracefully neglected.

'Miss Dinkarrao,' he said, going up to her, 'may I introduce Mr Axel Svensson, from Sweden. He is altogether interested in the story you were putting in your famous column about the ghorpad Yeshwant and his climbing feats.'

He let himself hope for a fleeting second that somehow the two of them might cancel each other out, or get together to talk endlessly about Shivaji and his ghorpad while he himself could get on with his business uninterrupted. But at once he abandoned the idea. It was too much to hope for.

'Mr Svensson, good afternoon,' Pinky said.

But it was to Ghote himself that she turned the full glare of her attention.

'Now, Inspector, what news? A new theft? A yet higher climb? More daring even? And some record price for whatever jewellery he has stolen?'

'No, madam. Unless I am hearing something when I am getting to my cabin, I do not think there has been a new theft.'

He sent a longing glance back over to the bat-wing doors through which he had hoped, just a moment ago, to pass into the familiar security of the cabin.

But he was not to get there yet.

'Well, you must tell me at once if there is something fresh,' Pinky Dinkarrao said. 'But

70

now I want to know what it is you yourself have been doing today? You are on the track of something? Yes? No?'

'No. No, madam, all that can be done just now is once more to ask questions of each and every victim so far of Yeshwant's daring climbs. I am not at all liking to intrude upon these ladies again. But it must be done.'

'So who have you just seen? Who are you going to see next?'

Ghote wondered whether he could say, *Police business*, but he knew how the majority of his colleagues all too soon abandoned that awesome phrase when there was a chance of seeing their name in print, accompanied if possible by the adjective *energetic* or the description *top-sleuth*. He could hope to fare no better, even if he was not so hundred per cent keen on getting into the papers.

'Madam, I have been attempting to interview a Mrs Gulabchand. But some difficulties are there.'

'Mrs Gulabchand-Investments Gulabchand? But I know her well, Inspector. She has been in my column many times. She is giving some very, very high-class parties. If you have a problem there, I can get her to see you in one second only.'

Ghote did not feel as grateful as he knew

he should. He had no doubt that Pinky Dinkarrao could secure *in one second only* with the lure of a mention in her column what all the authority of a Crime Branch officer seemed to be failing to obtain. But he wished it was not so. He knew it ought not to be so. He wished, too, now that he had been, as Axel Svensson had said he should have been, more determined in face of Mrs Gulabchand's vague promise of allowing him to go over her apartment when the demands of her social life permitted.

But, whatever the difficulties, he must get as soon as possible a good long look at the scene of Yeshwant's intrusion into the Gulabchand home, with Mrs Gulabchand there to question on the spot.

'Miss Dinkarrao,' he said, 'you are most kind.'

'I tell you what, Inspector,' Pinky answered. 'I will find out how soon Preeti can be free and then, if you give me your home number, I will ring you and we can meet at her place.'

'Most kind,' Ghote said.

He felt, however, that it was most unkind. Unkind of fate, if not of Pinky Dinkarrao. And there was, of course, worse to come.

'And Mr Svensson,' Pinky said with a flash of a smile on her intent features, 'since, as Inspector Ghote was saying, you also are interested in Yeshwant's activities, perhaps you would like to come. I am sure Preeti will be delighted.'

⋆　⋆　⋆

Ghote spent a frustrating afternoon devoted to trying to make his day's report to Deputy Commissioner Kabir sound more productive than it should truthfully have been. Then he had had an evening keeping an uneasy truce between his wife and his son — *Don't be pestering always*. Next morning he was, to his fury, almost late getting to the Taj to pick up Axel Svensson. From the hotel they were to go to Mrs Gulabchand's Green Apartments at Worli Seaface where it had been arranged in no time at all they would meet Pinky Dinkarrao at eleven o'clock.

Seething with impatience, he had found himself, shortly after ten, outside Churchgate Station unable to advance a single step amid the press of people heading for their places of work, latecomers every one. As was the custom, the crowds pouring out of the trains coming into the station — one every three minutes, packed to their open doors and beyond — were being held up in favour of the cars zooming past, their occupants equally leaving it till the last minute to arrive at their destinations. A long rope, attached to a post at the kerb and held at the other end by a hefty constable, kept the tumultuous newcomers in check.

Damn the fellow, Ghote had thought. Why can't he drop the bloody thing?

This, in spite of the fact that when by chance on other occasions he had been at this spot at much this time he had invariably thought to himself, Yes, we in the police do good sometimes. Crowds must be controlled.

However, at last the constable had let the rope fall and a thousand hurrying feet trampled over it to the far side, to surge into the chambers, offices and shops awaiting them. Ghote, pushing and elbowing with the best, managed to get over before the constable heaved up the rope once more.

In the event he reached the Taj at the exact time he had agreed with Axel Svensson. The big Swede was there in the lobby, wearing today in place of his white suit a smart blue shirt generously pocketed and decorated with innumerable buttons. At Worli Seaface, too, Pinky Dinkarrao, as ever carelessly wrapped in a highly coloured cotton sari, voluminous leather bag bumping at hip, emerged from a taxi just as they reached the tall, appropriately green-painted Green Apartments.

A servant opened the door to the ninth-floor flat at their ring of the bell. It was made abundantly plain then that this was a home where shoes were not worn inside. Once that had been explained to the looming, bear-like firinghi, they were ushered into the drawing room. Mrs Gulabchand, yet more imposing in a heavily hand-embroidered pink sari, was sitting supervising, beady-eyed, a man squatting at a low table re-stringing one of her pearl necklaces.

'Come again tomorrow,' she briskly told him. 'Leave that now.'

But, once the fellow had scuttled out, tea and dishes of sweetmeats had to be dutifully consumed, and praised, before Ghote felt he could put any questions.

'Madam,' he began at last, 'I was asking yesterday if I would be able to see exactly where was your valuable choker when this thief was laying hands on same.'

'It was in my bedroom, Inspector.'

'Yes, madam. So I may see the spot itself?'

'But it is my bedroom, Inspector. You are proposing to go in there to poke and pry to your full heart's content?'

Ghote blenched.

'Madam, it is necessary.'

He saw Mrs Gulabchand draw herself up.

He could not help then casting a glance,

even a beseeching glance, in Pinky Dinkarrao's direction. And the journalist's nose for
a story — *I See Mysterious Yeshwant
Unmasked* — overcame any shreds of
politeness she may have had.

'But, Preeti,' Pinky Dinkarrao said, 'you
must be knowing that the police have to go
here, there and everywhere. Into the slums,
into brothels, into matka gambling and
opium dens, everywhere.'

'My bedroom is not a — '

'No, no, Preeti. No one is suggesting that
your bedroom, let alone this apartment, is
anything at all like those places. I was just
pointing out that the police get used to being
in all sorts of homes. They take no notice.
They look only for what they need to see. For
clues.'

'And you are thinking they will find clues'
— a wrinkled nose — 'in my bedroom?'

'Well, if they are to get hold of this terrible
climbing thief they must first of all find some
clues. Where better than in a bedroom of a
home as well kept as this?'

The laid-on tribute to the splendour of the
apartment, and its state of pure cleanliness,
did the trick.

'Very well,' Mrs Gulabchand said.

Quickly Ghote got to his feet. Mrs
Gulabchand indicated that her journalist

friend alone should accompany him into the inner sanctum. They went.

And there was nothing to see.

Ghote re-examined the windows, now firmly closed to retain the big room's air-conditioned atmosphere. Long before this, he realized, the ledges under them must have been swept free even of every tiny grain of the fingerprint powder. He traced out next the path from windows to dressing table which Yeshwant must have crept along, noiseless as a ghost, while Mr and Mrs Gulabchand lay peacefully beside each other in the big bed. But each surface the fleshly bhoot might have touched was shining now from the efforts of a servant's duster-cloth.

'No good,' he said to Pinky at last.

'Well, I will at least be able to describe the very spot in my column. With all details.'

They returned to find Mrs Gulabchand telling Axel Svensson about the problems of living in the city.

'Believe me, Mr Svensson, whatever filth and dirt there may be in the road and even on the stairs in this block, I will not let it cross my door. Out there, filth. Inside here — '

Ghote ruthlessly interrupted. There was something he needed to clear up.

'Mrs Gulabchand,' he said. 'In your bedroom I was observing all windows were closed. This was to preserve cool from the A/C, yes?'

'Certainly, Inspector. Last year my husband was installing the very latest machines from Ajmani Air-Conditioning. They are most costly to run. So we are always keeping every window closed. It is shutting out noise also.'

'But then, madam, how was Yeshwant getting into your bedroom to take your choker?'

But, sharply though he had put the question, Mrs Gulabchand was unfazed.

'Of course, Inspector,' she said, 'at night, when it is quieter, I allow one window to be open. My husband is a Number One fresh air fiend, like a real Englishman Pinky was saying in her column once.'

One more hopeful line run into the sand, Ghote thought. One more rich lady interviewed to no purpose, too. What point would there be in asking to question the servants? Mrs Latika Patel's English-knowing guru had taught him that. There was no way any of them here could have informed Yeshwant that on just one occasion a valuable piece of jewellery had been left out of its safe, any more than there had been any way at the apartment at the top of towering Landsend.

Nothing else for it but to say goodbye. Taking Axel Svensson with him to put their shoes on again, he rang for the lift and descended, leaving Pinky Dinkarrao to extract from her friend some last morsels to enliven her column.

But it was while the two of them were standing in the lobby, bracing themselves to face the heat and noise of the city, that Axel Svensson said something that, in a moment, gave Ghote the lead he had almost lost hope of ever finding.

'Ganesh, tell me something about Mrs Gulabchand. Do you think she was hoping to get from some insurance firm more than the value of her stolen choker? I was remembering, when you put a question to her just now, that she had said out there at Juju Beach — '

'It is not Juju. It is Juhu. Juhu.'

'Yes, yes. At Juhu Beach. I was remembering that she was trying to claim that the choker was worth more than — what was it? — two something-or-others. And you were quoting to her the exact description you had from Pappy Chimanlal and Co. — '

'It is Pappubhai Chimanlal,' Ghote said, scarcely checking his exasperation.

Then the sudden thought came to him.

'Pappubhai Chimanlal and Co.,' he

repeated. 'Pappubhai Chimanlal and Co. Do you know, Axel, my good friend, I think at last I have seen something that can pinpoint this Yeshwant for me. Yes, I think that I have.'

6

No sooner had Ghote had that moment of illumination which the words *Pappubhai Chimanlal and Co.* had brought to him than, outside in the sun-hammered street, he spotted the yellow roof of a taxi. He went at a run through Green Apartments' heavy glass doors, calling back to Axel Svensson to come with him. What if Pinky Dinkarrao was to leave the flat on the ninth floor sooner than she might? What if she was to emerge from the lift — someone was jab-jabbing at a call button — while he was in the middle of telling Axel Svensson what had burst into his mind? If she got hold of the theory that had come to him about how Yeshwant operated, even though it was no more than an idea at present, she would seek to make it into a scoop for her column. Yeshwant would be warned. Then there would be nothing to stop him disappearing into the vast millions of India. The fellow must have made a huge sum already, even if, with the jewellery broken down and its gold settings untraceably melted, it would fetch no more than a tenth of its original value. But that would provide all the money any absconder would need, and more.

He succeeded in hailing the cab, and a moment later ponderous Axel Svensson, puffing more than a little, pounded up and joined him. They got in.

'Crawford Market,' Ghote ordered, thinking of all he might do at Headquarters to confirm the idea that had broken in on him.

Then, feeling he owed the firinghi an explanation, he risked being half-overheard by their Sikh driver. In as low a voice as he could he began accounting for what that spark of instant illumination had put into his head.

'Axel sahib, kindly do not be shouting out about what I am going to say. But it is thanks to yourself mentioning just now Pappubhai Chimanlal and Co. that something has come to me about Yeshwant. It is this: I am thinking that each and every one of the thefts I have so far investigated, and that is now almost all of them, was of a single maha expensive piece, just recently bought from Chimanlal's itself.'

'All from only that single — '

Then Axel Svensson managed to check his roar of sudden understanding.

'You are saying,' he went on in a heavy whisper, 'that Yeshwant is stealing only pieces of jewellery coming from this one place,

Pappubhai and Co. And that means — is this what your idea is? — that Yeshwant has access to that establishment. He waits until he gets to learn that some customer there has just bought a truly magnificent piece, and then, perhaps watching their apartment windows over some nights, he seizes his opportunity, climbs in and takes it.'

Under the rattle of the taxi's engine Ghote had not made out every word of the Swede's spit-splashy whispering. But, as he had been half-listening, he had begun to be swept over by doubts. When the idea had first struck him it had seemed so right that he had not even tried to find any flaws. Now he could not help asking if it was not somehow all too easy.

One of those doubts, barely formed in his head, was now unexpectedly put into words by Axel Svensson himself.

'But, listen, my friend. Something has just this moment occurred to me. Tell me, how is it that no one in all your Crime Bureau — your Crime Branch I ought to say — has not thought of this before? Perhaps you have not been told that inquiries at Pappubhai and Co. have produced some fact that spoils your theory.'

'No,' Ghote said, seeing what must have happened. 'No, at least that cannot be so. When I was being given my orders by Mr

Kabir, he would have informed. Definitely. No, what I think has happened is that it has not occurred to anyone that all the thefts are linked to Pappubhai Chimanlal and Co. because each of them up till I was put in charge was investigated by a different officer, most from local police stations, some in past few days only from Crime Branch. So no one has noticed this.'

'Yes,' Axel Svensson said brightening with every word. 'Yes, you are right. That is how it must have happened. There can be no doubt about it. But — But what a piece of luck for you, my friend that you have been so clever as to think of it.'

'Luck? What of luck?'

'That the circumstances were such that no one else was able to see the plain fact you have just hit on. If they had, before you were even given the case they would have found out who Yeshwant actually is and have put him behind bars.'

'Well, I am not altogether thinking that — '

'But, yes, my friend, yes. Now everything is in your favour. You have only to go to Pappubhai and Co. and make some hard-pressing inquiries and the whole truth will come out. There must be someone there who is feeding information to Yeshwant. Unless — Yes, unless Yeshwant himself is an

84

employee there. Yes, that is most probably it. Yeshwant is working at Pappubhai and Co. He is an employee. So, go there. Go and start asking questions. In five minutes or ten you will see a look on somebody's face that will tell you straight away you can make the arrest.'

'But, listen, Yeshwant may not at all be an employee at Pappubhai Chimanlal. He may be getting his informations just only from someone there, someone he is knowing. It may even be that this person is not at all realizing they are telling him what he is wanting to know.'

'No, no, my friend. I am sure Yeshwant works there. Certain. It is the most obvious explanation. No, tell our driver to go not to your Headquarters, but straight to — Where is that shop?'

'In Zaveri Bazaar. It is where all the big jewellers are.'

'Right. So you must go to Pappa-whatsit this moment. Driver, driver, go to Whatever-Bazaar. Top speed. Top speed.'

Ghote thanked his stars that the Swede's jumbled words had made no impression on the broad back and turbaned head of the Sikh at the wheel.

'No, listen,' he said urgently, taking Axel Svensson by the arm. 'Listen, we should not be in so much of hurry. If Yeshwant truly is a member of the staff at Pappubhai Chimanlal and Co., provided we are not charging into that place like some buffalo escaping from the dairies in north Bombay and causing utmost confusion, he can be safely left. He must not be allowed for any reason to guess the police is near to him. And it is the same if there is only some jasoos, some spy, of his in there. No, no. There is nothing to be done there just now.'

'But there is. There must be. You cannot discover what you have, and then sit back and do nothing about it. You cannot.'

But this, Ghote felt, was intruding too far into his own domain.

'I can,' he said. 'It is the right way to act. To do nothing whatsoever until more of certainty is there. And that is what I am going to do, to find out if what I have thought of is a certain fact.'

Axel Svensson turned away and humped himself into a large disapproving mass.

* * *

Ghote, when he had deposited his sulky companion at the Taj, realized that he could well be grateful that they had quarrelled. Now he could devote the rest of the day not to rushing like an invading horde into the calm of Pappubhai Chimanlal and Co.'s big air-conditioned showroom but, in Yeshwant's footsteps again, to checking the last of the places he had robbed and confirming, or not, that his victims had bought their jewellery from that most prestigious of firms.

So who is next on my list? he asked himself. Yes, it is one Mrs Shobna Parulkar. Husband is that well-known barrister, the very first of Yeshwant's victims.

Contacted on the telephone, Mrs Parulkar was happy to give him an almost immediate appointment. And, when he came to stand in front of the big old house off Cuffe Parade where the Parulkar flat was, he saw it would have presented no difficulty at all to climbing Yeshwant. The building was no more than five storeys high and its whole face was a mass of knobbly cornices and columns and balconies shaded by little sloping roofs.

Yes, he thought, even I would not have too much of a problem to climb up and up this old building to the top.

He went through the elaborate crumbling stone gateway. The chowkidar on his stool in the hallway was three-parts asleep in a state of faraway afternoon bliss. At a poke in the ribs, he blinked himself into a semblance of life and announced, with a grunt of malign pleasure, that the building had no lift.

'Kindly walk all way to top-top floor. There you would see bell of Parulkar memsahib's flat.'

Ghote tramped his way up, only pausing for a moment outside the flat to mop the sweat from his forehead and make a quick check of his notebook. Then the door was opened by a hunched old servant in khaki shorts and jacket, his duster over his shoulder.

'Memsahib is having pedicure,' the fellow said flatly. 'Mr Noronha is here.'

He seemed to be implying that any intrusion on his mistress at this sacred moment would be the equivalent of entering a temple in shoes.

'Go in,' Ghote said, feeling the sweat spring up again all down his back, 'and tell Parulkar memsahib Inspector Ghote is here, by appointment. Police inquiries cannot give way to any pedicures whatsoever.'

The man almost scuttled away. In less than two minutes he was back.

'Memsahib is saying, if Inspector sahib will not be minding Mr Noronha being at work, she is ready to see now.'

'Very well, take me to her.'

It was still a little lacking in respect, he felt, to want him to conduct his interview while the lady was having her feet attended to. But he was willing to make that sacrifice to advance his inquiries. The wife of an eminent barrister would be able, more likely than most, to provide clear details of the way her expensive pair of diamond karas had been stolen, even though the theft had been Yeshwant's first. It had been a sub-inspector from the nearest police station who had investigated months ago, and his report had been perfunctory at best.

He found Mrs Parulkar reclining in a lounging chair in her drawing room. One of her feet was resting on a towel on the lap of a kneeling, surgically white-uniformed Mr Noronha. The other was resting in a fragrant basin of warm water, its surface glinting with soapy bubbles.

'Inspector,' Mrs Parulkar said. 'You must forgive me. When I agreed to see you at this time I had altogether forgotten it was the day for Mr Noronha's monthly visit. But please ignore his presence altogether and ask me whatsoever you wish. Mr Noronha is the soul of discretion, I promise you. You are, aren't you, Mr Noronha?'

The Goan pedicurist looked up for one moment from his tender ministrations.

'Oh, I am discretion itself,' he said in tones as soapy as the water in the basin beside him.

'Not one word have I ever said about poor Mrs Parulkar's wonderful missing diamond bangles. Not one.'

It suddenly occurred to Ghote that unexpectedly he had a chance now to find out finally whether the theory that had come to him at Green Apartments was true or not. Rather than someone at Pappubhai Chimanlal's being the means whereby Yeshwant obtained his knowledge of where his rich hauls were to be found, it might be that this very man kneeling here was Yeshwant's informant. After all, the smarmy fellow would very likely pick up from his wealthy customers all sorts of gossip about their lives, including, if he wormed his way in, full boastful details of any new jewellery they had acquired.

More, if the fellow did turn out to be some friend of the unknown Yeshwant, it would put intrusive Axel Svensson's nose nicely out of joint.

'Are you having many customers you visit, Mr Noronha?' he asked in an idly conversational tone, going round to where he could see the man's face more clearly.

'Oh, no, Inspector. I go to a few precious customers only. Just people like Mrs Parulkar who fully understand how important it is to have truly beautiful feet.'

Ghote glanced at the foot Mr Noronha was cradling. It was slim and callus-free.

'But there are some other ladies you visit?' he asked. 'They are in this part of the city? Or do you go here and there to see them?'

'No, Inspector. All the ladies I go out to visit are at homes close to my little place, which is in Third Pasta Lane not very far from here, as you must be knowing.'

Ask the slimy fellow if Mrs Latika Patel, of Landsend, miles distant, was a customer?

No. End of road. It really was so unlikely that the man could go about all over the area Yeshwant had made his own that it was not worth pursuing. If the Goan had been Yeshwant's informant over the other thefts, he would never have risked claiming that none of the other victims was a customer of his. It could too easily be checked.

So, no. Pappubhai Chimanlal's loomed nearer, and a triumph for Axel Svensson.

But there were still questions to put to Mrs Parulkar. One in particular. But that, somehow, he wanted to leave for as long as possible.

'Madam,' he said now, 'when the investigating officer came after the theft of your karas, was he asking if you had noticed any signs of disturbance? Any signs at all? Some footmarks? Or perhaps Yeshwant, as he was climbing in, was leaving some threads from his clothes on the ironwork of your balcony?'

'Inspector, yes, I am good at noticing the smallest thing out of place, a ragged nail, a tiny wrinkle somewhere that can be made away with by some special cream I have, perhaps just a single grey hair. They can even come to a woman in her early thirties, you know.'

Ghote, who guessed Mrs Parulkar was well past her early forties, felt a growing impatience. Why would none of these wealthy ladies answer a simple question?

'Madam, if you are so noticing, kindly tell: did you or did you not see any signs left by Yeshwant?'

'Inspector, Inspector, don't press me so. Give me time to think. You know what you are doing? It is like what my little son is always saying to me, *Ma, give me some space.*'

Mr Noronha looked up a moment at this. A fleeting sly smile conveyed to Ghote that the *little son* had long left home.

'Inspector, if you give me some of that space,' Mrs Parulkar went on, 'then I may give you the answers you are seeking.'

'Yes, madam.'

He waited patiently while Mrs Parulkar lay back, deep in thought to judge by eyes hidden behind delicately kohl-darkened eye-lids. There seemed to be no frown lines of concentration on her smooth forehead, however.

Minutes passed.

At last she spoke.

'Mr Noronha, you dear man, don't you think it is time for the other foot now?'

'Madam,' Ghote broke in. 'Have you remembered even one small thing out of place after Yeshwant's intrusion?'

'Oh, yes. Yes, that awful person. But, do you know, Inspector, I don't think I have noticed anything. I am afraid I cannot possibly help you.'

Ghote sighed.

So now that question which he wanted and did not want to hear answered had to be put.

'Mrs Parulkar, I find it is failing to state in the report Sub-inspector Mathur made where it was that you were purchasing your beautiful karas. Please, for final details, can you tell me that?'

But it had been a mistake, in trying to ensure her attention, to have put in that word *beautiful*.

'Yes, Inspector,' Mrs Parulkar said. 'Yes, how true. There is nothing that enhances the beauty of one's hands, if one is gifted with hands of a certain elegance, than to wear beautiful karas on one's wrists. Each sets the other off.'

And, for his special benefit, she held out both her long-fingered hands, decorated at this daylight hour with no more than bangles of simple gold, and gave them each a graceful twirl.

'And you were purchasing those stolen karas where, madam?' Ghote asked, now with a sharpness he could not suppress.

'It was my husband who bought them, Inspector. A twent — An anniversary gift. He went, of course, to Pappubhai Chimanlal, Inspector. That is much the best place to go.'

So, yes, Ghote registered. More support for Axel Svensson's too-enthusiastic backing of my own idea. Should I even take this as conclusive? Go at once to Zaveri Bazaar? Do as Axel Svensson suggested, make some noisy inquiries, all the while keeping one eye out for signs of guiltiness?

No.

He pulled himself up.

No, I must not let the firinghi's unprofessional enthusiasm run away with me. I said I would ask and ask of Yeshwant's victims till the list of possible Pappubhai Chimanlal customers is one hundred per cent complete, and I will do it. There are, in fact, now two more names only to be asked. There is that

Punjabi lady staying in a block called Sea Scape at New Marine Lines, Mrs Shantilal Mehta, wife of a senior executive of Peshawar Pharmaceuticals. And there is the lady I am so far failing to see in the Bombay Hospital, Mrs Marzban. If both of these have been Pappubhai Chimanlal customers, I will have to admit to my pushing and pushing Swedish friend he was right, and go to there straight away. If one of them fails to be, I will not expect to find Yeshwant so easily.

Mrs Marzban I must leave as long as possible. After all, she would only just be recovering from whatever operation she was having, some 'nose-job' as they are calling it or some excess fat perhaps to be cut away. But perhaps now I can try to see if Mrs Mehta is at home. Then I can talk to her without any interferences from my Swedish friend or, as bad, Miss Pinky Dinkarrao.

But, interference or no interference, I will find Yeshwant.

Somehow.

7

Ghote, standing in New Marine Lines outside *The Blossoms* English-medium school for small children, looked across at Mrs Shantilal Mehta's yellow-painted, smooth-faced, modern block, Sea Scape, scene of the most recent of Yeshwant's exploits. Sea Scape, he thought. How many apartment blocks in the city seized on the word *Sea* for their names? Sea Dream, Sea Foam, Sea Land, Sea Site, he had seen all of these one after another when he had left the old house where the Parulkars lived. And there had been an Ocean View as well. With all the buildings that had come up in recent years, not many of the people in those sea-named places could have nowadays much more than a twisted glimpse of the sea. Yet each name spoke of the longing to look out over far-stretching water with all its promise of escape into peacefulness from the city's ever inward-breaking turmoil.

Not that you needed a distant sight of the Arabian Sea, he thought, to feel at times, to feel almost all the time, that longing for unpressured peace.

Never mind all that, there was work to be done.

Mrs Mehta's drawing room, he saw as he entered it, was very different from the softly feminine one where Mrs Parulkar had offered her elegant feet to her pedicurist's attentions. Nor was it much like the richly decorated and scrupulously clean room from which he had gone for his privileged view of Mrs Gulabchand's equally clean bedroom. Nor, again, was it like the one where Mrs Patel, nested in her huge brocaded armchair, had until her husband erupted on to the scene devoted herself so completely to her baby. Mrs Mehta's drawing room was — no other word for it — filmi. The furnishings might all have been carried off from the sets of one of Bollywood's most elaborate song-and-dance films. On the wall to the left of the door there was a lifesize statue of an apsara, voluptuously full-breasted as only a celestial maiden could be, naked save for a few jewelled ribbons. On the opposite wall a huge bright red refrigerator thrummed and shuddered. Four large and glittering chandeliers were dispelling the early evening dark. Glossy calendars, some with pictures of the gods, one with a photo of a swimsuited woman holding up a huge tube of Peshawar

Pharmaceuticals' Hand-protection Cream, hung here and there. An enormous gold starburst clock proclaimed that it was five minutes past six.

Mrs Mehta, robustly handsome in a brilliant orange salwar kameez, was standing underneath the two furthest chandeliers. Ghote went up to her. A heavy cloud of perfume, he found, surrounded her like a defensive sphere. Into his mind there came the voice of his mother telling him, time and again, the story from the *Mahabharata* of the thirteenth day of the great battle between the Pandavas and the Kauravas when Drona, leader of the Kauravas, had arrayed his forces in the impregnable lotus formation, which only Abhimanyu, son of Arjuna, could penetrate.

However much in those childhood days he had pictured himself as brave Abhimanyu, now he felt he was by no means such. Nevertheless, he advanced into the perfumed aura. Time once more to dart out the questions he had asked so many times since he had been given the Yeshwant inquiry.

'Madam, it is concerning the theft of your diamond ear-tops. The police is hoping that this thief they are calling as Yeshwant can be laid by the heel if we are able to find out how he is getting to know such items as your ear-tops were within his reach. So, madam, first I must be repeating the question Inspector Adik from Crime Branch was putting to you. He was writing in his report that you were altogether certain your servants would not have talked to anyone about your jewelleries. Can you be confirming same?'

'My servants?' Mrs Mehta replied. 'Yes, Inspector, I can tell you absolutely that not one of them could be the person who was passing to Yeshwant that I always kept my jewels in the drawer beside my bed. All our servants are Punjabis who have been in our family their whole lives, and came on with us from Delhi where my husband was last posted. They hardly speak any Hindi, and not a word of Marathi.'

Ghote was about to thank her for being so directly informative. His next question, the vital one about which jewellers had supplied the ear-tops, was in his head waiting to be asked. But suddenly something in the way Mrs Mehta had replied struck him as not quite right.

Not one of her servants, she had said, *could be the person who was passing to Yeshwant that I always kept my jewels in the drawer beside my bed.* But this meant surely that there was someone who did know where her jewels were kept and might have told Yeshwant.

'Madam,' he said, 'who then was it who was informing Yeshwant of this?'

He was afraid he had been too blunt. But the look of cautious calculation on Mrs Mehta's handsome face as she chewed with lipstick-stained teeth at her full lower lip told him that bluntness might be about to pay off.

'Inspector . . . '

'Yes, madam?'

'Inspector, I have a confession to make about this matter.'

'Yes, madam?'

'Yes. When that other Crime Branch officer came . . . '

'Inspector Adik, madam.'

'Yes. Adik. I remember now. When Inspector Adik asked me if I could suggest how this Yeshwant fellow had got to know about my ear-tops, I first of all asked him if he was sure no one from Pappubhai Chimanlal and Co. could have passed on information that I had just acquired them.'

Pappubhai Chimanlal's once more. One other victim only now to be asked. Well, if it was so, it was so.

'Yes,' Mrs Mehta went on, 'Inspector Adik was at once laughing to scorn that idea. All right, he was saying some employee at

Chimanlal's may have known about my purchase. But how could they know the ear-tops were in my bedside-table drawer? He was asking that in very sharp manner.'

Mrs Mehta stopped, and looked over at the round-breasted apsara on the wall, as if hoping for guidance from swarga above in what she still had to say.

'Inspector Adik is one first-class officer,' Ghote prompted, though in fact he had always believed Adik too ready to be aggressive in his questioning.

'Yes, yes. That is what I was afraid of.'

'Afraid, madam?'

'Yes. Afraid that Inspector Adik would find out what I was not, at that time, at all wanting anyone to know.'

'And that was what, madam?' he asked, with all the quiet carefulness he could muster.

'It is what I have to confess to you now, Inspector,' Mrs Mehta replied, flicking a glance of gratitude out to him. 'When I was talking to Inspector Adik I was just managing to throw some dust in his eyes by mentioning servants as passing on information. But he questioned me about mine then, and very soon it came out, as I have told, how they are speaking hardly anything but Punjabi.'

Again handsome, self-confident Mrs Mehta fell silent.

'Yes, madam,' Ghote said. 'But you told you were going to confess something to me.'

Am I being too much like Adik?

'Inspector, do you have any brothers?' Mrs Mehta said abruptly.

Ghote blinked.

'No, madam, no,' he answered. 'Sisters I am having, but no brother.'

'Then perhaps you will not find it easy to understand what I am going to tell you.'

'Madam, I would try.'

'Inspector, I do have a brother. A much younger brother, but he was the first son in the family.'

'Yes, madam?'

'Perhaps you know how the first son is always so much apple of the parents' eyes. Always, you know, there is a danger he will be spoilt by too much of tenderness, by too much of not correcting faults.'

Again a silence.

'And this was what was happening to your brother, madam?'

'Yes,' she answered. 'Yes, Harilal is a spoilt brat. That is the truth.'

Ghote took in a breath. This was the moment.

'And it is your brother Harilal who, you think, may have informed Yeshwant where were your diamond ear-tops?'

Ghote's first reaction — he cursed himself that it was so — was that this put an end to Axel Svensson's claim that Yeshwant must be a Pappubhai Chimanlal employee. He ought, he knew, to be regretting that a hopeful line had proved a dead end. But he did not.

'Madam,' he said, 'if, as you are stating, your brother would pass on to this thief Yeshwant where your diamond ear-tops were to be found, why would your brother not be stealing same himself?'

'Ah, no, Inspector. Harilal would not dare take my ear-tops when it would be evident to me, and to my husband also, that he was the one who had done it. No, he must be the person who was just only passing on this information to Yeshwant, whoever he is, seeking to be given his share of proceeds.'

'I see, madam. But kindly state: why did you not tell Inspector Adik all this? And why are you telling myself now?'

Mrs Mehta again bit at her full lower lip.

'It is quite simple,' she said eventually. 'When Inspector Adik was here I believed that Harilal's new videos store was being a great success. He was saying and saying it. I thought we had done at last with his borrowing and never paying back, with his sometimes making off also with something here that he could sell. Yes, he was always

103

doing that, Inspector, my brother. It was for his gambling and fast living. But then, just only after Inspector Adik was here, Harilal was coming once more and wanting me to get him money. He was threatening that the family would be disgraced if it came out he had bought the stock for his new shop without having wherewithal to pay for it, when also we had already given him funds for that itself. Well, I was begging my husband, and he was agreeing once more to pay up. But he was saying, *Last time*. And I was knowing from the way he said it that now Harilal had gone too far. And I, too, was hardening my heart to say it. No, if Harilal was the one to tell Yeshwant about my ear-tops, I am ready now to see that bad hat stand in court.'

There was a tear, Ghote could not help noticing, in the left eye of the self-assured, perfume-protected woman who had stood under the glitteringly lit chandeliers to greet him.

'Madam,' he said, 'I think I have no more questions.'

But one he had. At the door he turned and asked it.

'Madam, you are knowing I must learn where is your brother Harilal's shop?'

At once Mrs Mehta strode over to the

side-table facing the voluptuous apsara. She jerked open its drawer with such force that the heavy gold cigarette-lighter on it fell to its side. From the drawer she snatched a dark blue leather-bound address book. She scrabbled for a moment at its pages and then thrust it under Ghote's nose.

Harilal Tandon, he read, *Video Valley — Subash Chowk, opp. Rajasthan Emporium.*

He thought it best to leave without another word.

★　★　★

Video Valley, he found half an hour later, was more of a stream-trickling nullah than any sort of valley. Small, even tiny, the shop had a long upright slab of grained stone for its façade with *Video Valley* cut into it in letters of gold. A brightly lit display window next to this made up for its narrowness by the size of the film poster that was its sole ornament. The sound of loud Western music was thundering out from its half-open door.

Trying not to let the thumping rhythm penetrate, Ghote advanced into the hostile territory.

A young man with no more than a hint of a moustache was leaning moodily on the glass counter staring into total vacancy. Hardly the smart proprietor of this smart, if unpaid for, establishment.

'Mr Tandon, he is available?' Ghote asked him over the thump-thump-thump of the music.

'Inside.' And a yawn.

Ghote saw there was a door at the far end. Without another word, he marched up to it and thrust it open. He found he was in an office that was little more than a cupboard. But at the desk, a telephone clamped to his ear, was the man who must be Mrs Mehta's bad-hat brother.

'Inspector Ghote, Crime Branch,' he banged out without ceremony.

Harilal Tandon dropped the telephone as if it had suddenly turned into a deadly snake.

'Crime Branch,' he choked out.

'Yes,' Ghote said. 'And I am thinking a Crime Branch officer is a person you would very much like not to be seeing.'

Harilal Tandon began to recover a little. He picked up the phone and put it back on its rest.

'But — But why should I mind whoever I am seeing?' he said.

Ghote put a small grim smile on to his face.

'Because, Mr Tandon, you may have something to hide. Something not at all legal.'

'No. No.' A gasp for breath. 'Why should you think that?'

'Perhaps because I have just been talking to Mrs Shantilal Mehta, your sister.'

'Shantilal? What — What has she been saying about me? It's a lie. Yes, she has never liked me. And now she is doing her level best to get me into trouble.'

'I am more thinking that it is yourself who has been getting you into trouble.'

Harilal Tandon looked from side to side. But nowhere in the tiny office was there anything that might help him.

'What — What sort of trouble are you — Are you meaning, Inspector?' he muttered at last.

'Well, I am not concerned with your financial difficulties,' Ghote told him.

The reassurance did not seem to bring him any great comfort.

Ghote reckoned the young man had now been made to worry enough.

'You may still help yourself, Mr Tandon,' he said. 'You have only to co-operate fully. So, tell me the real identity of your friend who is going by the name of Yeshwant.'

'Yeshwant? Yeshwant?'

Harilal Tandon looked plainly bewildered. He swallowed. Once.

'Inspector, are you talking about that fellow

the papers were making such a tamasha about? The fellow who got into my sister's bedroom while she and her pig of a husband were snoring and made off with her famous diamond ear-tops?'

This was not what Ghote had expected.

He stood looking down at Video Valley's owner retaining as much as he could of his unyielding expression. But through his mind there raced a whole squadron of questions. Had Harilal Tandon simply managed to pull himself together enough to make his brazen denial? Or could he really know of the name Yeshwant only as something he had casually read about in newspapers? Was his picture of Mr Mehta, snoring there like a pig, made not because Yeshwant had told him about it but out of mere passing spite? Was Harilal Tandon really not in any way hand-in-gloves with Yeshwant? And, if he was not, did that mean Axel Svensson was after all fully right?

And gradually the answers formed themselves in his mind.

Yes, it might be possible that this bad hat had somehow become acquainted with the man whose daring climbing burglaries had earned him the name Yeshwant. But, even if that were so, how could Video Valley's owner have got to know where a stranger to him like Mrs Parulkar kept the karas she believed

108

made her hands still look elegant? How could he have known where Mrs Gulabchand laid down her two-lakh choker when her fresh air loving husband had been allowed to open their bedroom window? What could have told him, when Mrs Patel in the late stages of her pregnancy had left her sapphire necklace out, that she had done so? Let alone how could the fellow have obtained all the other information that had helped Yeshwant to commit his burglaries?

No, nothing else for it but to acknowledge that Axel Svensson was most likely in the right when he insisted that the path to Yeshwant must lie through the Zaveri Bazaar establishment of Pappubhai Chimanlal and Co.

8

Next morning there were no reports of a new
Yeshwant robbery. So Ghote, informed that
Mrs Marzban could see him 'if inquiries are
really necessary', set off on his scooter for the
Bombay Hospital. But he found the monotonous throbbing of its engine was not for once
sending him off into *his Northern fastness*.
Perhaps, he thought, it is just only because
peak-hour traffic is so bad today. At any one
moment I may be knocked to ground.

A zooming little white Maruti brushed so
closely past him that the sleeve of his shirt
was almost whipped from his arm. Recovering, he reflected that, even if he was not safe
in his own world here, at least last night there
had been no more *Swabhimaan* versus *Lost
in Space* trouble, if only because Ved
complaining once more of mental harassment
had gone out without so much as sitting
down to eat.

Or, he added to himself glancing warily at
the speeding cars behind, perhaps I cannot
feel the contentment I had before Svensson
sahib was breaking into my life again because
I am still feeling the fellow is invading my

mind with that belief of his that Yeshwant must be a Pappubhai Chimanlal employee.

As if it was not the idea I myself was having first, even if now I feel somehow it is not right. But, yes, definitely it is best not to go to Zaveri Bazaar yet. I cannot be finding arguments for what I feel, nothing that would make that firinghi change his damn Swedish mind. But all the same I am believing somehow, somehow, that Yeshwant being at Pappubhai Chimanlal and Co., quietly going about his business, is not the right sort of answer.

So let me hope Mrs Marzban, recovering after her nose-job or whatsoever it was, in that private bed, Cabin Number 17, will say altogether definitely she is never buying jewelleries from Pappubhai Chimanlal.

But — wait — here is the mosque with outside it the big rack, ten shelves high, twenty metres long, where worshippers are putting their shoes. Almost opposite hospital itself.

He brought his scooter to a halt and manoeuvred it off the traffic-mad roadway. There was, he saw, a huge old banyan nearby, its dangling dried-up brown roots forming a sort of open curtain all round, and right inside its wide-split trunk a beggar had made a little home for himself, safe from any final monsoon showers that might yet break out. Rags and poverty, but a picture of faraway peace.

Or is he after all some sort of holy man, cross-legged in meditation? He may be. Or he may be a man just lost in his own thoughts, remembering perhaps days when he had had a wife, children, and had been happy. Or when he had had a nag for a wife and noisy demanding children and had been miserable.

In any case, don't break in on him and ask him to look after the scooter while I am inside. Let him stay in his lost world while he can.

*　*　*

Shown by a white-capped ward boy into Cabin 17, Ghote was instantly aware of the sharp odour of liberally sprinkled eau-de-cologne. But the sight that confronted him on the white iron cot in the centre of the room brought him to a shocked halt. He had been expecting to see a spruce widow, recovering well from a minor operation. But Mrs Marzban, lying propped on a heap of pillows, looked like nothing so much as the remains of a person once active and alive, a rag doll in a white hospital gown.

A twenty-year-old nurse had at his

112

entrance quickly put down the paperback *Lost in Love*, in whose pearly pink world she had been immersed.

Lost in Love or *Lost in Space*, he thought. What is there of difference?

'Nurse, I am Inspector Ghote, Crime Branch,' he snapped out. 'I was informed Mrs Marzban would be able to answer some questions. But now I am asking if I have not come too late.'

'No, Inspector, no,' the girl said unconcernedly, 'patient is not too bad. She has been sleeping only. If you talk, she will soon answer.'

In some trepidation, Ghote approached the hygienic-looking cot. There was a hard little metal chair beside it. He sat himself down, and realized immediately why the cabin had been so lavishly sprayed with eau-de-cologne. From the bandages on each of Mrs Marzban's wrists there was coming the unmistakable smell of putrescent flesh. He saw, too, on the arm nearer him, into which the long tube of a saline drip had been inserted, a whole series of little blue-black bruises from where she had been given injections.

Poor woman, he thought, perhaps in the last stages of life to be brutally invaded by the steel prong of the drip, by all those needles.

'Mrs Marzban,' he said quietly.

No reponse.

He gave a little sharp cough.

'Mrs Marzban?'

The eyelids in the skeleton head flickered.

'It is you, Behram?'

The words, faint but clear as water, issued from the parched sunken lips.

Ghote did not know what to say. Who was this Behram he was being mistaken for? Not a husband. He had been told Mrs Marzban was a widow. Some dear relative? How should he disillusion this death's-door woman?

But, in response to his silence, at last she turned her head further in his direction.

'No.' A sigh, or a groan. 'No, not my Behram . . . He said he would not come till afternoon . . . And it must be morning still . . . Is it? Is it morning? Poor Behram, how he hates seeing me like this.'

My Behram. So definitely not a relation.

'Yes, madam, it is morning,' Ghote said, for want of anything better.

In the skull-like head with its wisps of remaining hair the eyes widened now. Ghote saw they were after all alert with questioning intelligence.

'So, if you are not my lover, who are you?'

'Your lov — ' Ghote brought out, not a little shocked at the blatancy of the dying

114

woman's question.

He recovered himself.

'Madam, I am Inspector Ghote, from Crime Branch. I am here — They told me I could come. Come to put to you — Madam, I have to ask — I would like to ask certain questions about the theft from your home at Meher Apartments of a valuable diamond ring.'

'Poor Behram.'

That, it seemed, was all the answer he was going to get. Mrs Marzban appeared to have slipped back totally into the deep drowse in which he had first seen her.

He sat in silence. Despondency at her sad state overwhelmed him. Nor did he know what to say in response to that name Behram. If he was ever to be called on for a response. Had she truly said *my lover*? Truly?

But at last his silence was rewarded.

'That was the ring he would give me,' the stricken woman on the cot said, adding murmured syllable to murmured syllable. 'Knew my life was over. Still insisted on . . . insisted on giving me that toy.'

'Madam, I am talking of a ring that is not at all a toy. Madam, I am understanding it was very, very valuable. A diamond ring as valuable almost as it is possible to have.'

There came a curious sound from the bed

then. It took Ghote some seconds to realize it was a laugh.

'Oh, yes, very, very valuable, Inspector. It is Inspector?'

'Yes, madam. Inspector Ghote.'

'Well then, Inspector, think about this. Ask yourself who paid for that very, very valuable diamond ring. Do you think it was a poet, a poet who even when he was famous and writing every day could hardly pay for the cigarettes he smoked? A poet who for years has lived on just the memory of those poems? Lived sozzled, happily sozzled, on the gin I keep for him? No, I was the one who paid for that present, Inspector. I paid. Who else?'

'Yes, madam.'

What else could he say? If Mrs Marzban really had a poet as her lover and if that poet had spent the last many years happily, as she had said, *sozzled*, then who but she could have bought her own diamond ring?

Or was all this that a woman in the last stages of illness was saying nothing but imagination? Did she really have a lover? And was that lover a poet? Or was this, like the romance the careless nurse in the corner had gone back to reading, a mere dream?

Try to pin it down? Ask something that connected what she had been saying to the actual theft by climbing Yeshwant, from the

116

sixth floor of Block A at Meher Apartments? If this interview obtained with such difficulty was to lead anywhere, something like that must be asked.

And, if it is answered, will it lead on to the question that damned Swede keeps putting into my head? *Is every one of Yeshwant's thefts linked to Pappubhai Chimanlal and Co.?*

Try.

'Madam, can you kindly be telling me when it was diamond ring in question was purchased?' He drew in a quick breath. 'And where also, madam?'

'Oh, yes. Yes. It was stolen, wasn't it, that silly ring? After all our fights about buying it. That man . . . The climber . . . Yes, Yeshwant. He climbed all the way up, up to the apartment. Romantic. Romantic, too. Nearly as romantic as my poor Behram. He should . . . write a poem . . . '

And silence.

After a little Ghote even felt obliged to lean forwards to make sure those had not been the poor woman's last words.

He was confronted by eyes suddenly wide open again.

'When? When? Inspector, didn't you know that?' A new silence. 'It was a birthday present for me. And, poor impulsive poet that he is, Behram could not wait till the day. I suppose he thought in his heart of hearts I would never reach it. And I suppose I won't. Even though his gift has already been stolen. By that Yeshwant. Yeshwant, the climber, yes.'

Ghote sat further back in his uncomfortable little chair.

'So, madam,' he said, 'kindly say when exactly this birthday gift was purchased? And where also?'

'Oh, if it is so important to you to know . . . I can very well remember going with Behram to buy it. I had to go, you see, because I had to be there to sign the cheque. My poor poet.'

'So, madam, when?'

'My birthday is October the thirty-first. In a few days, yes? Though I'll hardly be here to celebrate. So then, it must have been on September the first, two exact months in advance, that we went to buy it. There, Inspector, one fact-fact for your police officer's notebook.'

So, she was realizing all along I was suspecting this-all was a dream only. But, yes, I can rely on that date as a fact now. Then what about the next fact? The fact of where?

'Madam, where it was it you made this purchase?'

'Zaveri Bazaar, Inspector.'

118

'Of course, madam. But at which jeweller?'

Now. Now it would come.

And come it did. With complete conviction. Overwhelming conviction.

'At Karamdas and Sons, Inspector.'

9

Leaving death's-door Mrs Marzban, sunk once more into an uneasy half-sleep, and her attendant nurse back safely again in her pearly pink world of *Lost in Love*, Ghote could not help feeling sharp pleasure that he had clung to his irrational doubts about Yeshwant being a Pappubhai Chimanlal employee. However it had come about that the discriminating thief knew that Mrs Marzban had signed a cheque for a valuable diamond ring, it was plain now that he could not have learnt it sitting in Chimanlal's workshop or standing behind a Chimanlal showroom counter. No, if Yeshwant was to be tracked down, it was not going to be at the Zaveri Bazaar jeweller's premises.

For a moment he was tempted to ride his scooter at once to the Taj to tell Axel Svensson what he had found out. But then something made him hesitate, perhaps that same caution which had kept him from acting immediately on the Swede's assertion it was certain Yeshwant worked for Pappubhai Chimanlal.

Had there been an indefinable something

not quite right about what Mrs Marzban had said? Some illogicality? Something out of place among the words she had, out of her state of desperate illness, poured on to him in jabs of unconnected thought? It would be worth a lot to have some solid confirmation of all the things she had said. How far away from reality was she? No use asking little Head-in-a-book in the corner of the ward. The doctor in charge? But he might not know enough about her mental state to be able to produce a really definite answer.

And then he realized there very likely was someone who would know.

Her poet lover would surely be able to say whether that this-way, that-way transaction over her birthday gift had or had not taken place. Nor should there be much difficulty in getting to see the fellow. From what Mrs Marzban had said it was plain he shared her flat at Meher Apartments.

Go there.

Go there straight away and find out what other name than Behram the fellow had. Mrs Marzban had murmured that he was going to visit her in the afternoon. This did not necessarily mean he would be in the apartment now at nearly noon. But it was not unlikely.

Heaving his scooter off its stand in front of

the old beggar's niche in the ancient banyan, Ghote settled himself on the saddle, fired up the engine and started off.

It was in the end all his little machine could do to get up the winding hill of Altamount Road and on to the twin block of apartments where Mrs Marzban had her flat. But at last, while it was still not much past midday, it brought him there. Only, as he tugged the machine on to its stand in the shade of a deep green mango tree, for him to hesitate once more.

What had there been, as a matter of plain fact, in what Mrs Marzban had said to cast doubt on her having purchased that diamond ring at Karamdas and Sons? She had brought out that name clearly and directly, even forcefully. So why not take her at her word? And there was also a certain problem about going up to the sixth-floor flat and trying to see the poet lover. Could he ring at the bell and ask for *Behram*, just like that? What if the servant said, *Who Behram?* And what if, even if he got to see the fellow, he turned out to be so *sozzled* that no sense could be got out of him?

He stepped back into the mango tree's shade, half-determined to mount his scooter and go. But, as he did so, the long row of garages behind the blocks caught his eye.

Each had, he saw, a boldly painted number above it.

He went over. Looking along the row, he soon enough spotted 62, the number he remembered from the First Information Report of the theft. And, more, its metal shutter was raised and from the interior music was coming, a radio or something playing holy bhajans.

So, someone there inside. Who else could it be but Mrs Marzban's driver? Unless it was the sozzled poet himself, not perhaps very likely. But from the driver he might learn whether Behram existed, what his full name was, how worthwhile it would be to approach him.

The garage was almost entirely filled by a big dark blue Contessa. Beyond it a man in driver's uniform was simultaneously idly polishing the already immaculate car and worshipping at a bazaar picture of Lord Ganesh, under which two or three agarbattis were perfuming the air with their grey-blue smoke. The music of the bhajans was, he realized, coming from a tape inside the car.

A sharp cough was enough to bring the driver out of his smoky religious haze.

'Sahib?'

'Inspector Ghote, Crime Branch.'

Although the man had not looked appalled

at hearing his name and rank, as a good many in his position would have been, Ghote was pleased to note he showed at least a swift tinge of apprehension.

'Inspector. What — What are you wanting?'

'You are Mrs Marzban's driver?'

'Jee haan, Inspector. For seven-eight years, and not one complaint. Not one even.'

'So you will be able to tell all I am asking.'

'Jee, Inspector.'

Yes, he thought, the fellow will tell me anything whatsoever. He has heard what happens to servants under police custody when they are suspected of a crime, or even when they are not. I am not at all thinking that is a hundred per cent fine thing. But it has its uses.

Like now.

'Mrs Marzban has had a long-time lover,' Ghote shot out at the driver, scarcely making it a question.

'Jee, Inspector. He is Shri Behram Bottlewala.'

Ghote saw he was being given a quick appraising look. The fellow was wondering whether he could venture to be indiscreet. He produced for him a faint expression of dislike, as if he was one of the people prejudiced against all Parsis.

'Bottlewala by name . . . ' the driver said, watching him.

124

And saw that he had said enough.

So Mrs Marzban, poor sick woman, had not been imagining for herself a happy life that she had never had. Her poet lover did exist, and was clearly often *sozzled*. So, he truly had, as she had said, given her a very valuable diamond ring as an advance birthday present, and she really had paid for it herself. But had she paid at Karamdas and Sons?

Why did he still feel there was something wrong about that emphatic statement of hers? There was nothing really to indicate it was not the straightforward truth. Yet he still felt it somehow might not be.

'Mr Bottlewala is at home now?' he asked, putting an ice-sliver of coldness into his voice to make it plain that servants speaking ill of their employers was not something an inspector of the Mumbai Police wished to hear.

'Jee, Inspector,' the subdued reply came. 'Bottlewala sahib not ever leaving apartment till late in afternoon.'

'Right. Get on with your work.'

Ghote swung away.

Up on the sixth floor of Block A, he scarcely paused before ringing the bell on the door of Apartment 62. A servant promptly answered.

'Mr Bottlewala?'

'Yes, sahib. He is at home. What is your good name, please?'

'Inspector Ghote, Crime Branch. In connection with the theft here of a valuable diamond ring.'

'Yes, sahib. Terrible thing. That Yeshwant, climbing so high.'

The man gave a shudder.

No, plainly one servant who was not the daring and discriminating thief's informant. In any case, even if he had been, how could he have informed Yeshwant about all the other robberies here and there over the city?

'I will tell Bottlewala sahib,' the man said now, and padded bare-footed away.

He returned almost at once and led Ghote into yet another rich drawing room. One, he felt from a brief glance, not basically unfamiliar. It was typically Parsi. Ancient furniture intricately carved in dark rosewood loomed from the walls. Heavy little tables, equally dark, were everywhere. Glass-fronted cabinets gleamed with the items of silver half-hidden inside them.

Items of silver, easy to carry off, he thought. But none of which Yeshwant had taken. Why, he wondered. Why?

But no time to ponder that now. Standing beside an open, very untypically Parsi, chromium-decorated drinks cabinet was a short, elderly-looking individual, face sloppily round, belly lolling out beneath a finely embroidered Lucknow kurta, the thin gold chain round his neck almost lost in its folds. The poet lover. And, if not sozzled now, showing all the signs of that state being habitual.

He introduced himself.

'Inspector,' the poet said, 'I was just making myself a little drinkie. Can I get you one? You know, a spot of gin in the middle of the morning does wonders for one's outlook. Away dull care. That's the thing.'

'No thank you, sir.'

The sozzled poet shrugged.

'Your choice, Inspector. Well, perhaps I'll do the drinking for you. Only decent thing.'

He poured a very generous quantity of gin into a tumbler. And swallowed it.

'That's better. Now, what can I do for you, Inspector?'

'Sir, I have just come from the Bombay Hospital where Mrs Marzban was good enough, in spite of her most poor health, to answer to a certain extent some questions it was my duty to ask.'

'Most poor health? Most poor health? My darling Dolly is dying, Inspector. Dying. Dying, Egypt, dying.'

'Sir, I much regret such was also seeming to me.'

'Nay, madam, I know not seems.'

What on earth was the fellow saying now? Yes, sozzled indeed.

'Sir, I will be brief.'

'As woman's . . . No, no. Never mind a wretched old poet, Inspector, just ask. Ask and ye shall be answered.'

Ghote swallowed.

'Very good, sir. Then kindly tell where it was Mrs Marzban was buying the ring this fellow Yeshwant was stealing. Sir, was it from Karamdas and Sons?'

All right, it was asked. Before anything else. Now for the answer.

The poet laughed.

'Oh, my God,' he said. 'My poor Dolly. She has really gone out of — Oh, my poor, poor Dolly.'

The laugh, hardly ended, turned into tears flooding down limp, sagging cheeks as the poet slumped into the nearest heavily carved armchair.

Nearly answered, and now this. Would that answer never come?

Ghote turned away and looked out of the nearest window. The view of the far-stretching city was certainly wonderful. And, yes, he could see the sea, the peaceful sea, with, beyond its sun-glinting surface, on the far side of Back Bay the dark silhouettes of the tall office blocks of Nariman Point, close-packed as if they had been heaped together from a child's playbox and churning out their facts, figures and fancies to enter into the heads of every man, woman and child in the city's thirteen million inhabitants.

He stood where he was, trying to pretend he was not even there, while the sound of the poet's gurgling sobs went on and on.

And then were checked.

''Nother drinkie. Dull care.'

There came the sound of gin being poured, if anything more generously than before.

Ghote ventured to turn back.

'Sir . . . The ring. At Karamdas and Sons?'

'No, Inspector. No, no, not at all. You see, we had one of our fights about just that. Dolly has never bought any jewellery at Karamdas and Sons. But I had heard that better bargains are to be got there. So I suggested I buy there the diamond ring I wanted to give her. Well, that she should buy for me there. But, no, she absolutely insisted on going to the showroom she had always been to even as little more than a girl.'

What showroom? Could it be . . . ?

Ask then. Ask.

'Sir, what place was this she was always going to?'

One last tear slid down the poet's baggy left cheek.

'She got them mixed up, you see, when she talked to you, Inspector,' he said. 'Her poor mind just switched the two over.'

'I see, sir.'

Ghote fell silent. It seemed the least he could do.

A minute passed. Another began.

'It was Pappubhai Chimanlal and Co., Inspector.'

So, yes, right to have felt instinctively that something had been wrong about dying Mrs Marzban's assertion. Perhaps, looking back, it was because the ramblingly incoherent woman had made her assertion with too much conviction, too overwhelmingly. As if she had been issuing a challenge. As she had been. She had been challenging her sozzled lover over his choice of Karamdas and Sons as the place to buy the ring. But because her last fight with the man she loved had meant too much to her, she had switched the two shops over in her mind. She had somehow come to believe the ring had been bought at Karamdas and Sons as the poet had wanted. It had not. It had been bought at Pappubhai Chimanlal and Co.

* * *

Rescuing his scooter from under the mango tree, after leaving Mrs Marzban's lover once more enclosed in his sozzled world, Ghote realized it was much darker under the tree's shade than before. He looked up at the sky. Yes, a rain cloud had come up seemingly from nowhere, and it looked very much as if at any minute they were to have a heavy shower, perhaps the last one of the monsoon. And he was wearing no more than a shirt and trousers.

Stay where he was? Or risk a wetting?

He had seen himself, in so far as he had been able to plan ahead at all, once more grabbing a midday bite from the banana-laden handcart of a thelawalla. How much more comforting, he had thought, than all the air-conditioned luxury of the Taj buffet. But now he felt he owed it to Axel Svensson to admit at once that every one of Yeshwant's victims had in fact bought from Pappubhai Chimanlal and Co. their stolen pieces of jewellery.

Risk a wetting to make his admission? Well, perhaps he ought to submit to such a punishment. Retribution. But to enter the cut-off, air-conditioned splendour of the huge hotel soaked to the skin like a drowned kitten? Must he do that? Dripping all over its floors and carpets?

Well, yes, perhaps he owed his inward-pushing, aggressive friend even that.

10

It seemed that the gods had decided to reward Inspector Ghote. Though the rain did come pouring down on to him, it lasted, like most late-monsoon showers, only a few minutes. By the time he arrived at the Taj to make his confession to Axel Svensson his shoulders were no more than a little damp. In the buffet his Swedish friend, back in his white suit again, was also in a magnanimous frame of mind.

'Yes, yes, my good Ganesh. Your idea that someone at Pappubhai and Co. must be the person who is telling Yeshwant where fine hauls of jewellery are to be found is altogether justified now. So — I have eaten all I want here — shall we go at once and see what some sharp words will produce? You may even have your hands on Yeshwant himself in half an hour from now, if my notion is right that it is the man himself who sits there like a spider.'

A spider, Ghote thought. Yes, and one that every so often goes climbing up and up a long thread from its web to where high above it is seeing some juicy fly. But will I really pull this spider from his web? Am I in fact on the point of doing so? At the Zaveri Bazaar showroom of Pappubhai Chimanlal and Co.?

As they sat in the taxi going there, Ghote thought he ought now to enquire of Axel Svensson what he had been doing to amuse himself since he had left him the day before. He recollected, with a pang of conscience, that his friend had been in something of a sulk after being told in effect to keep his big Swedish nose out of his own affairs.

'So, Axel, how has it been with you?'

The Swede gave him a grin, somewhat shame-faced yet not without a tinge of pride.

'Not altogether good,' he said.

Ghote felt a jab of dismay. What now? The firinghi caught by another touting guide with a new horror story? Even on their way to a possible confrontation with mysterious Yeshwant was the Swede going to tell him something that would demand his immediate attention?

'So what it is?' he asked, almost breathlessly.

'Ah, well, it is over now, thank goodness. But at the time it was — Well, it was pretty scary, to tell you the truth.'

Over? So perhaps nothing to be dealt with just now. But would such a piece of luck really come to me?

'But, Axel, what was happening? Tell me.'

Another grin.

'I was in a riot.'

'A riot? But what riot? Where it was?'

There was almost always a riot of some sort somewhere in the city. But Ghote could not recollect having heard of anything major.

'Where was it, Ganesh? Well, I hardly know. You see, early last night I decided I would take a nice long walk. I love to see the life of the streets, you know. The people so cheerful and smiling, the noisiness and the bright colours everywhere, even in the dark. Mumbai or Bombay, this is a lively city.'

'Yes, yes. But . . . ?'

'Well, as I say, I do not know really where I was. But there was a cinema there. It seemed to be showing a film called *Fire*. And at first I thought it must be something very popular because there was a big crowd outside, looking as if they were pushing to get in. So I went forward to take a look.'

'But it was not only tickets they were wanting,' Ghote said, suddenly realizing the sort of mess Axel Svensson must have got himself into.

Fire was a notorious film, the first in India, a few years back, to show lesbian lovers. It had, of course, outraged opinion then from one end of the country to the other. Such women could not exist in a good Hindu land. They never had. They never should. Wicked Western imperialists were attempting to invade the sacred country once more, if not now with troops with vile propaganda for inadmissible matters.

There had been letters in the papers then pointing out that all this was not altogether true. But there had been mobs in the streets who saw to it that the film was withdrawn, to be shown only in religion-less countries across the black sea. And now, it seemed, an attempt was being made quietly to bring out the film again. If what Axel Svensson was saying was an accurate account, at least one new riot had already been caused. In which the big Swede had been caught up.

'But Axel, Axel sahib, were you hurt? Were you injured?'

'No, no. I was not. Or only a little. A few bruises. My best shirt was torn.'

So that was why the white suit was on show again.

'You are sure? How were you escaping? Did you see the hotel doctor afterwards?'

'No, no. That was not necessary. Not at all. But, yes, I was escaping. I was escaping, I am sorry to say, by pushing my way out and running away as fast as I could.'

'No, no. You were quite right. Sometimes a

mob like that can go so far as to tear an enemy limb from limb. I was telling you, two-three days ago, how the Shiv Sena is ready to fight and fight to keep Maharashtra a good Maharashtrian state. No invasions, whether it is of southerners from India itself or people from the West bringing in their Western ways. No, if it was those people protesting there, you were hundred per cent right to get away as fast as you could. But you ought not to have plunged into an angry crowd like that, you know.'

'Well, in the end no harm was done,' Axel Svensson said, seemingly the better for having told of his adventure.

No harm done? Well, perhaps there had not been. But . . . But had the Swede, conspicuous as he always was, somehow aroused the enmity of the stop-at-nothing hangers-on of the Shiv Sena? Was there trouble somewhere ahead?

But at least there was none at present. Nothing between this moment and — could it be? — the moment when he would lay hands on Yeshwant?

The taxi drew up outside the glintingly smart exterior of the Pappubhai Chimanlal and Co. showroom.

Standing in front of one of its heavy glass doors, his hand on the big dark-engraved metal handle, the bustle and loud talk of Zaveri Bazaar in his ears, Ghote found he was by no means as full of optimism as the tall Swede behind him about their chances of coming face to face with the man he had been ordered to find.

All very well, he thought, to be throwing looks of suspicion towards each and every employee who may come under my eye. But still there may be some other way for Yeshwant to have learnt about the fine jewellery that is seeming always to attract him. Look, here right by my side there is this vendor sitting on his stool, his tray on its stand in front of him, busy rethreading the beads on a necklace for that fat housewife, her keys hanging from her waist. It may be possible, if a fellow like this is keeping his ears open, to overhear what customers coming out of the showroom are saying. *I am thinking I was getting one bargain there, a marvellous pair of diamond karas for less than a lakh.*

It might be.

But, no. No, the fellow could sometimes pick up a scrap or two of talk, but he could never have overheard precise information about each one of Yeshwant's victims. Too good to be true altogether. Another fine idea dead before it had truly come to life.

So . . .

So the first person I am seeing when I am pulling at this big handle and hauling open this door may be Yeshwant himself.

But the first person Ghote did see when, the Swede at his heels, he had gone through the door and the down-draughting air-curtain beyond into the cool, dust-free, almost antiseptic atmosphere of the big showroom was, beyond any doubt, not Yeshwant. He was a man sitting at the very rear of the showroom, wearing only a simple white churida kurta. But there was such an air of solidly aggressive confidence about him, from the broad dome of his bald head to the thrust of his nose, the determinedly downward turn of his wide mouth and the steady set of his heavy shoulders, that he altogether eclipsed the suited, tie-wearing assistants behind the room's ranks of showcases. Ghote had no doubt this was the establishment's long-time proprietor. He was — he must be — Shri Pappubhai Chimanlal himself.

As Ghote came up to the wide glass table behind which Pappubhai Chimanlal was seated, he saw on its black velvet-backed surface a scatter of glittering diamonds, with beside them a little silver jeweller's loupe, a silver instrument for holding the tiny gems, a decorative tin of chewy, spicy paan masala and a multi-buttoned white telephone.

So this is it, he thought. Not at all the time for suspicious looks to everyone I am chancing to see. The time now to ask Shri Chimanlal directly who can have been telling Yeshwant, the master thief, about the expensive-expensive purchases made here over months past.

'It is Shri Pappubhai Chimanlal?'

'Yes.'

The heavyset Gujarati looked up at him.

Hard to tell whether this was just a blank statement of affirmation or something with a hint of an enquiry in it.

Ghote chose to believe the latter.

'Mr Chimanlal,' he said, 'I am Inspector Ghote, of Crime Branch. I am making inquiries concerning the thefts committed by the man the press is calling as Yeshwant.'

'So?'

'Mr Chimanlal, you must be aware that it is pieces of Pappubhai Chimanlal jewellery that have been stolen.'

'What if?'

'But perhaps you are not aware, sir, of what my full inquiries have revealed. Each and every one of this Yeshwant's robberies has been of jewels recently purchased from this showroom itself.'

The jeweller looked up at him, his heavy face even more sombre than before.

139

'So, what for are you telling me this, Inspector?'

Ghote, feeling as if he was pushing and pushing uselessly at some soft but unyielding massive substance, forced himself to lean forward more sharply over the diamond-studded table.

For one quick moment he thought how easy it might be to put his hands flat on the black surface below him and come away with one of those tiny chips of immensely valuable — What was it he had once read they really consisted of? Yes, crystalline carbon.

'Sir,' he said, back in an instant to the police officer, 'were you all along knowing that each of Yeshwant's thefts was of a Pappubhai Chimanlal jewellery?'

A look of calculation on the broad face below him. But a fleeting look only.

'No, Inspector. No, I was not. The newspapers were not always mentioning where this Yeshwant's thefts had been bought, also they were not giving proper descriptions. They are using only ridiculous expressions, and ridiculous sums of rupees also.'

At last some sort of acknowledgement.

'Then, sir, I must repeat. Rigorous inquiries have shown that none of the thefts which the said Yeshwant climbed up to commit were of jewels other than from your establishment. Sir, I ask: what is that meaning to you?'

A silence. The silver pick-up tool, grasped in podgy, be-ringed fingers, was shifted a little to and fro.

'Yes,' Pappubhai Chimanlal said at last. 'It might seem to show this Yeshwant has some means of knowing what is sold from this shop.'

'Some means, sir, of finding out in utmost detail what is sold from this shop. You must be knowing that Yeshwant has never stolen anything that was not worth a very great deal of money. Only one theft of his, I am able to tell you, was bringing him nothing. But that was because the lady in question had had the good sense to place a diamond necklace, bought from you, sir, into her safe.'

'Very well, Inspector. Yeshwant has some good means of knowing about the more valuable sales we are making.'

'So, sir, the question is there. How is he knowing such? Sir, may I interview each and every one of your employees?'

'No, Inspector.'

At this rebuff Ghote felt, rather than saw, Axel Svensson moving up behind him. Quickly he put in his own word.

'Sir, howsoever important is an establishment like yours, police inquiries must take precedence.'

'Must, Inspector?'

The jeweller let go the little silver tool he had been fiddling with. But before Ghote had brought himself to mention the article of the Indian Penal Code that set penalties for obstructing an officer of the law, Section 186, Pappubhai Chimanlal produced something that might have been a conciliatory smile.

'Inspector, let me explain the workings of this establishment, which you have been good enough to describe as important. We are handling here gold, diamonds and other jewels worth, shall we say, almost as much as the revenues of the Maharashtra State Government.'

His eyes dropped to the array of dozens of glittering little diamonds in front of him.

'So, Inspector, it becomes necessary to have certain rules and procedures.'

He glanced up now with a sudden hard and hostile look.

'For example, Inspector, if it should have occurred to you, standing where you are, to dip your hand down and take one of these diamonds in front of you, one worth perhaps your whole year's salary plus increments, do you think you would be able to leave these premises with it dropped into your shirt pocket?'

'I am supposing not, sir.'

'You are supposing correctly, Inspector. Before you had so much as turned round I would have put my foot on a button under the table here, and those doors behind you, and every other door in the showroom, would have been fast-locked.'

'Very good, sir,' Ghote said, inwardly flushing with gladness that his tiny wicked thought of a minute or two earlier had been no more than a tiny wicked thought.

'Other precautions also are necessary, Inspector. Every valuable piece in the whole showroom has to be accounted for at all times. Any information about them is always kept as strictly confidential. No employee may discuss any sale they are making with any other employee. I myself, of course, conduct all sales that are coming over a certain value. So, you see, Inspector, questioning, as you said, *each and every one* of my employees will be unnecessary. It would also make them angry. So, Inspector, it is *No.*'

Ghote stood for a moment considering what Pappubhai Chimanlal had said. Had those arguments of his been put simply because he did not want his staff upset? Or had they been valid in themselves?

He had still not answered that in his mind, as Pappubhai Chimanlal sat solidly looking up at him, when he became aware of what seemed like a heavy storm cloud gathering force at his shoulder. Before he could do anything to check it, it broke.

'Mr Pappubhai,' Axel Svensson boomed out, 'you are not behaving in any sort of correct manner.'

Ghote turned.

'Axel sahib — '

'No, I must say it. Mr Pappubhai — '

'Svensson sahib,' Ghote jabbed out. 'Kindly be silent.'

And this frail umbrella did succeed, more effectually than his wishes had done during his scooter trip from Meher Apartments to the Taj, in holding back the deluge.

He thought it best, however, not to attempt to explain the intrusion to the jeweller.

'Yes, sir,' he hastily said to him, 'I am altogether appreciating the reasons you have stated. I no longer consider it necessary to put questions to your staff.'

He swirled round to the firinghi.

'Come, Axel.'

But then, perhaps because the big Swede seemed ready to block his path, he turned back again.

144

'Mr Chimanlal, one thing more only.'

'Yes, Inspector?'

The jeweller looked up from the diamond he was already beginning to scrutinize through his loupe.

'Sir, can I have your full assurance that there is no one whatsoever among your staff, even down somehow to the sweepers, who may for any reason have knowledge of all transactions taking place here?'

Pappubhai Chimanlal slowly took the loupe from his eye.

He gave Ghote a long hard look.

'You are right, Inspector,' he said at last. 'There is someone. Yes. No sooner had you turned to go than I realized that to a certain extent I had misinformed you. I did not, however, think it worth putting right my mistake.'

'Sir, but — '

'However, thanks to the foreign gentleman who seems to be with you, the opportunity is now there.'

Ghote hardly knew whether to feel gratitude to Axel Svensson or not.

'So, sir . . . ' he ventured.

'Yes, Inspector. There is my secretary, Miss Cooper.'

'And she is knowing all your business affairs, sir?'

The solidly heavy face rose up to meet his eyes. There was a gleam of sullen determination on it.

'Yes, Inspector. She is, how do they say, my right arm. Everything she is knowing. Everything.'

'Then, sir . . . '

'No, Inspector.'

'But, sir, if as you are stating Miss Cooper is only one besides yourself who is knowing what-all happens in this showroom, then, sir, if someone is telling this Yeshwant where are the owners of items sold from here, sir, it must be Miss Cooper.'

'It is not, Inspector.'

'Sir, why are you knowing this with so much of certainty?'

Ghote began to be afraid that Axel Svensson, still within hearing though he had now stepped back a pace, would again come blundering in.

He could think, which was worse, of no way of stopping him.

Luckily, however, the jeweller answered his question in an altogether milder tone.

'Inspector, Miss Cooper has been my secretary for more than twenty years. She is coming next to my wife. I can be sure of her loyalties always.'

'Yes, sir. But all the same it is still seeming

that somehow through her Yeshwant must be gaining his informations. Sir, Miss Cooper is here? May I see?'

'No, Inspector.'

'But, sir . . . '

The shrewd eyes in the heavy big face looked up at him again.

'Inspector, what you were saying is your name?'

Ah, here it comes. *A word to the Commissioner, and you will find you are no longer able to go question-questioning people who have no time for such.*

'I am Inspector Ghote, sir.'

Get ready for battle.

But Pappubhai Chimanlal said something very different from the customary threat.

He lowered his voice, almost to a thin growl.

'Inspector. Get rid of that foreigner, whoever he is.'

What is this, Ghote thought.

But without hesitation he turned to Axel Svensson. If this influential witness wanted the big Swede not to hear what he was going to say, the big Swede had to go. Find what excuse to him he could.

'Axel, my friend, I think you had better step outside just now.'

'But — '

'No buts and butting, please. Go only.'

There must have been something in his tone that told the Swede he had to do as he had been asked.

'Well, I will see you shortly, my friend.'

'Certainly. Yes, yes. But go now.'

Axel Svensson went.

Ghote turned back to Pappubhai Chimanlal.

'Sir?'

'Mr Ghote, you are a man of world?'

Only one answer.

'Yes, sir.'

'Then let me tell you a story. Once upon a time — That is the way the English begin their stories, yes?'

'Yes, sir.'

'Then once upon a time there was a young shop-owner in this city. Young, but wanting to make the small business his father had left to him get bigger and better. So, first of all, he was doing what anyone like himself should do. He was marrying a wife who came with some dowry, not too much but enough. Yet she came with that only. A girl of a good Gujarati family, in same line also, but not too much educated. No college-bollege. So, one knowing jewels, yes, but nothing of business-fizziness. But this young man was determined still to make himself one day rich-rich. About business-fizziness he also was not knowing too much. But about other things he had already learnt all he was needing to know. So what was he doing next? He was getting as secretary, confidential secretary, an educated Anglo-Indian girl, first class with letters-writing, account-keeping, tax and legal matters, as the Anglo-Indians are if they are having good education. For some weeks this young man was watching her and watching her. He found she was a lonely girl, Miss Ivy Cooper, not at all experience. No lover-dovers. Good church-perch Christian girl. So then, when he was satisfied he knew all about her, what do you think he was doing, Mr Ghote?'

'I do not know, sir.'

'Perhaps you do not. Perhaps you do. But what he was doing, even though he was having one good Hindu wife, was one night keeping that girl late, late in office. And at last having. Once and once only having.'

Ghote had almost asked: *Having?* But then he realized what the young Pappubhai Chimanlal had done to the young Ivy Cooper. He had seduced her. Ruthlessly but cleverly. And once and once only. And thereby he had ensured himself for as many years as he wanted of a lastingly loving, absolutely loyal secretary.

'Sir, a one hundred per cent interesting story. Thank you, sir.'

An interesting story. But one that told him, as clearly as could be, that he was not going to be allowed to go to any office at the rear of the big showroom to interview Miss Ivy Cooper.

He looked down at Pappubhai Chimanlal, already with a paan he had taken from the pretty round tin at his elbow sloshily moving between his jaws.

'Then, sir, I will be going now,' he said. 'Once more, thank you.'

And through the big glass doors he went.

But as they swung closed behind him he made a vow.

By hooks and by crooks, I am going to find out where is staying Miss Ivy Cooper. I am going to ask her many, many questions. And she will be answering. Howsoever much she is still loving her boss.

11

Ghote found Axel Svensson wandering like a great lost bear among the crowd in Zaveri Bazaar. Shoppers were shopping, and window-gazing. Teaboys were swinging their six full milky glasses in their wire baskets. A sadhu was wandering past, lost in his own world. A little group of posh girls, jeans tight round their legs, headphones clamped to their ears, were walking through, oblivious of everything, everyone and each other. Hand-cartwallas were hurrying by pushing their long, loaded carts, *Way please, way please*. A pair of students, cloth bags stuffed with books, were idling along, talking hard to each other regardless of anyone else. Coolies with their odd and immense head-loads, a TV set, a rolled-up mattress, were making their way past, seemingly ignoring the weights pressing down on them.

'Axel sahib,' Ghote called out. 'Axel sahib.'

The big Swede turned, and gave Ghote a look, sullen as a reprimanded schoolboy.

'Axel, I must be apologizing for making you leave like that. But, kindly believe, it was most necessary. Chimanlal sahib was feeling he was not able to speak freely before a foreigner. When I tell what I was learning you will see.'

'Well, what was it?'

At once, rapidly as he could, he gave the Swede the gist of Pappubhai Chimanlal's sideways-on explanation of how, though his secretary knew everything about his firm, she could not possibly have passed on any confidential information.

'But Miss Ivy Cooper I am going to see,' he concluded. 'It is seeming to me it cannot be anyone else whatsoever who is giving Yeshwant what he is wanting to learn.'

'No,' Axel Svensson shot out, still distinctly belligerent.

'No, you are saying? No?'

The Swede gave him a grimly triumphant smile.

'It is not the secretary miss who is passing to Yeshwant the information he requires,' he said. 'Shall I tell you who it really is?'

Ghote found all this hard to understand.

'Kindly do,' he said.

Axel Svensson turned round and pointed dramatically back towards the showroom he had been so unceremoniously turned out of.

'There,' he said. 'There. There is your man.'

After a moment Ghote realized he was

pointing at the bead-stringing vendor, sitting idle now on his low stool beside the showroom's shining glass doors.

His felt a sharp little sinking of depression. How was he to explain to his Swedish friend that he had jumped to a totally wrong conclusion?

'Axel sahib,' he said. 'That is, Axel. Axel, what you have guessed is very clever. Up to a point. But I am afraid it is no good. I, too, was surmising about that fellow. But, you know, no one sitting just only where he is could have heard at twenty different times — and remember Yeshwant has stolen nearly twenty maha valuable jewelleries — the exact informations he has had.'

The crestfallen look on that long ago bony face hit at him. Oh, why, why, had he let himself be saddled with this forlorn firinghi, breaking in on him at every turn with his difficulties and disappointments? But he had. And he must do what he could for him.

'But, listen, Axel,' he jabbered on. 'Listen, I would very much like your help and assistance this evening. I am going, if I possibly can, to see Miss Ivy Cooper at home. She may be the one chance I am having of getting near to Yeshwant and all his thievings. And — And — '

He thought hard.

'And, yes, she is an Anglo-Indian, you know. And their English is not always too easy for me to understand. So to have someone from the West with me would be one very great advantage.'

It was nonsense. But it seemed to work.

Axel Svensson straightened his broad shoulders and looked up as if an enemy had suddenly sprung to life before him, waiting to be conquered.

'So, you would be ready if I am coming to Taj at nine p.m. itself?'

'Ganesh, I will.'

★   ★   ★

When shortly before nine that evening Ghote entered the huge Taj lobby, softly radiant beneath its chandeliers, its hostesses in their gorgeous saris tall and aloof behind their long counter, he found Axel Svensson already there, sitting alertly on one of the many deeply plump pink sofas.

'Ganesh, Ganesh,' his voice rang out, for every guest and visitor to hear. 'Ganesh, have you found where Ivy Copper lives?'

Ivy Copper. Ivy Copper. Why cannot this damn Swede ever get any name right? And this is an English-sounding one, and he is meant to speak that language altogether as well as myself.

But I suppose I must be grateful that he has at least misnamed the suspect I am going to see. At least no one here in the lobby, where all the world, all the world of the rich at least, is at some time coming to sit, will have recognized who he was shouting about.

'Yes,' he said, going up to the Swede. 'Yes, I have found Ivy Cooper's address. It is in a colony out towards Andheri where many railway workers stay. You know almost all engine-drivers used to be Anglo-Indians, right from British days? Many still are.'

'Very good, very good,' Axel Svensson said, rising to his feet. 'But how did you find her out so quickly?'

Ghote grinned.

'Simple. I was thinking that her boss would insist she had a phone. I looked her up. And there she was. Are you ready to go?'

'Yes, yes. You know, my friend, I am willing to bet you will bring your inquiry to a close well before your fellow officers on the Amjani case.'

No, Ghote thought. I must not let him get wrong every name he is uttering. *Mr Pappubhai* was bad enough, and *Copper* he will perhaps change for himself. But now is the time to say something.

'Axel, my friend. You are making the same

mistake you were making before. It is not Amjani: it is Ajmani.'

Something that might have been a blush showed itself on Axel Svensson's ample cheeks. Quickly Ghote found a sweetmeat to offer to this baby.

'But,' he said, 'I have something to tell about that case. When I was finding out that phone number at Headquarters I was learning also that Inspector Adik, over at Shanti Niwas — '

'Shanti Niwas, that is House of Quiet?' the Swede broke in.

'It is House of Peace. Shanti is Peace. Peace.'

'Oh, yes, yes. I will remember now.'

'Over at Shanti Niwas,' Ghote said, a touch coldly, 'Inspector Adik has discovered the murder weapon. So we will have to be lucky-lucky if we are to find Yeshwant before Adik is putting his murderer behind the bars.'

'But what was that weapon?' the Swede said. 'Is it really a good clue to the man who used it?'

'It may not be a man,' Ghote said, with a little laugh. 'You see, the weapon Adik was finding — it was thrown into a fountain in the gardens there — was a fish knife.'

'A fish-knife? A fish-knife? But that's one of those things old-fashioned families in Europe use. Made of silver, from the days when steel knives gave a bad taste to fish. Quite blunt. No good at all even for cutting up meat.'

Ghote laughed again.

'No, no. I did not know such things as that existed. But this is very much different. It is a knife for gutting fish. Very sharp. Used by fishwallis anywhere along the coast round here when their men are bringing in the catch.'

'Ah, not a fish-knife, but a fish knife, ja.'

'And if that is perhaps indicating who used it, it should be a woman. But, though those fishwallis are tough as one old boot and well capable of using their knives for nefarious purposes, getting into the heart of Anil Ajmani's house was hardly a woman's work.'

'No, I suppose not. Not if the place is as doubly secure as you were saying the other day. So, perhaps we are first in the race after all. Let's go then. Let's go and see your Miss Ivy Copper.'

'Cooper, Cooper.'

★ ★ ★

It was raining again when Ghote and Svensson arrived in Andheri, a faint almost imperceptible drizzle, quietly persistent if hardly penetrating. Their taxi had brought them to somewhere near the address Ghote had got for Miss Cooper. Somewhere near only. Being armed with an address in the huge sprawling, divided and subdivided city is seldom enough to get you precisely to where you want to go. So it was only after half a dozen inquiries that they had got even close.

But eventually they arrived at a small compound formed by four rows of two-storey buildings. It was in an Anglo-Indian area where Ivy Cooper's flat ought to be located. It looked at first as if the whole compound was deserted, though the tinny sounds of Western pop music were coming from here and there in the surrounding buildings, and lights, yellow or blueish, could be seen in many of the barred windows.

But half under the shelter of an almost leafless gul mohar tree near the solitary street lamp in the centre of the compound Ghote spotted an old man, a typical Anglo-Indian, fairish complexion, white hair, dressed only in a torn singlet and khaki shorts. He was sitting in an ancient canework peacock chair, the wide fan of its back brokenly leaning to one side. In front of him, on a square of thick cardboard resting on an empty drum of vanaspati cooking-oil, cards were laid out for what looked in the feeble, rain-smeared light to be a game of patience.

Perhaps this man could point them at last to their destination.

'Good evening,' Ghote greeted him, noting that all the time he had been there not one of the greasy, tattered cards had been moved. 'I am looking for Miss Ivy Cooper. Can you tell me where she stays?'

No reply.

Ghote tried again, repeating his own words in a much louder voice.

But the old white-haired Anglo-Indian simply sat, unmoving, looked down with apparent intentness at the cards on his sagging cardboard sheet as the faint rain gradually soaked it.

Is he hundred per cent deaf, Ghote wondered. Or has he like my father, and myself sometimes, retreated altogether into *his Northern fastness?*

Cautiously he reached forward and tapped the old man on his bare shoulder.

The action did produce a response. A hand reached out and moved a card from one pile to another.

'Not there,' Axel Svensson boomed.

He had been at Ghote's elbow looking down at the spread of cards, and appeared to have worked out the rules of whatever game it was.

'No, you should put the queen of diamonds there, not the queen of hearts.'

And it seemed that the big Swede's loud correction had penetrated like a band of marauders right into the old man's fastness.

'Queen of hearts best, man,' came a muttered growl, as if not the intruder but some fellow cards-player of years ago was being contradicted.

At least, Ghote said to himself, the fellow can hear, and speak.

He moved round to a point where under the lamp's pale light his shadow fell across the sodden board.

'I am looking for one Miss Ivy Cooper,' he said.

He must at last have made his voice forceful enough to pierce, like Axel Svensson's, through to the old man's head. Because he looked up.

'Miss Cooper?' Ghote repeated, even more forcefully. 'Ivy Cooper?'

'Getting me dinner.'

Now Axel Svensson must have thought the time for his role as interpreter had come.

'He is saying Miss Cooper is getting him some dinner,' he whispered to Ghote, adding a less authoritative, 'I think.'

'You are related to Ivy Cooper?' Ghote asked the old man, pushfully penetrating still.

No reply once more.

But two cards were moved in rapid succession, apparently with Axel Svensson's approval.

But then the old Anglo-Indian did lift up his head and address Ghote directly.

'Lazy cow's dad, aren't I?' he muttered.

Ghote was more than a little surprised to hear Ivy Cooper, praised by Pappubhai Chimanlal as the woman whose business talents he relied on, described as a lazy cow. He wondered what the Gujarati jeweller would say if he knew he had confided his secrets to someone her own father could dismiss in this way.

And then he wondered something more. If Ivy Cooper really was a lazy cow, could it be that she had plans to ensure for herself in the end a long life of laziness by getting her share of Yeshwant's booty?

The moment had come, he thought, to cease to be the bothersome stranger breaking in on an old man's self-absorbed pleasure and to become the police officer making demands backed up, if need be, by the plain threat of the lock-up.

'Mr Cooper,' he banged out, 'I am a police officer here in pursuance of duty. I am requiring to see your daughter, one Miss Ivy Cooper. Where will I find? Now?'

And memories of days of discipline, far, far

away, seemed to make their way into the old man's limited area of awareness.

'Police,' he muttered. 'Bloody police . . . always . . . '

'Where?' Ghote snapped.

The old Anglo-Indian turned a little in his broken chair and pointed at one of the doors on the second-storey balcony, the finger at the end of his bare, rain-wetted arm a wavering up and down.

Ghote swung away and started out.

Behind him he heard Axel Svensson attempting to placate Ivy Cooper's life-exhausted father.

'Mr Cooper . . . It is, I assure you, urgent business. Yes, urgent. And . . . and, please, try putting that queen of diamonds under the king of . . . '

But the old man had entered his own world again.

Axel Svensson just managed, going at a shambling run across the muddied-over compound and up the wooden stairs to the balcony above, to catch up with Ghote as he made a hard-knuckled fist and knocked a sharp tattoo on Ivy Cooper's door. It opened, letting out a tangy, oily smell of frying.

Revealed in the intermittently flickering light coming from a defective tube-182light, Pappubhai Chimanlal's devoted secretary looked to be about forty. Her flat-chested, awkward frame was unbecomingly dressed in a brightly colourful flowered frock of the sort that most Anglo-Indian women carry off with more sexual swank. On her lightly pock-marked face, the bold ruby-red frame of a pair of spectacles was her sole attempt at adornment.

'Miss Ivy Cooper? Inspector Ghote, Crime Branch.'

Had a look of alarm come on to that past-mending plain face?

Yes, Ghote thought, all those years ago young Pappubhai Chimanlal knew what he was about when he set out to give a taste of the delights of love to his new secretary whose chances of ever knowing them must have seemed small enough.

But, with the light, such as it was, coming from behind her, let alone the fact that the wide lenses of her spectacles were still misted over from her stove, it was impossible to detect what change if any had shown itself on her face at the words *Crime Branch*.

So, forcing her back into the flat's hall, as the living room in such places was called, Ghote pushed his way in.

'Madam,' he said, striding across and ruthlessly switching off the TV burblingly issuing some science-fiction episode, all people with odd-shaped ears and mechanical-sounding voices, 'I am making inquiries in connection with certain thefts carried out by one known as Yeshwant.'

Certainly now there was some reaction. Ivy Cooper's pale lips tightened.

But was it actually because the name Yeshwant cut deep with her? Was she in fact preparing herself to deny ever giving anybody any information about Pappubhai Chimanlal and Co.? Or was she no more than aware, as perhaps Pappubhai Chimanlal himself had been all along, that each of Yeshwant's thefts had been of something particularly valuable recently bought at the showroom? And had she simply wondered how this could have come about?

Ask. Ask directly. Break into any defences she has made for herself.

'So, madam, I am asking: have you at any time described to any individual whatsoever items sold from Pappubhai Chimanlal and Co.'s showrooms?'

She jerked back.

'No.'

The look from behind the ruby-red spectacles was all defiance.

'Madam, I am suggesting that is what you have done. Who was it to? Madam, you have a brother?'

'No, Inspector, no, no.'

'I am able to ask your father out there in the compound, madam. No use to try any lies and lying. Do you have a brother? Even one who long ago left home?'

'No. No, man. Why should I lie to you? I have no brothers. I never did have. You can ask my father, if he's able to bring himself back from thinking he's driving his old loco or checking his Hon. Sec. books of the retirees club. You can ask him all you want.'

'Then, madam, you are having some cousin? Some cousin you are very much liking? Some cousin you are very much wanting to see become a well-off fellow?'

'No, Inspector. No. What are you saying? What are you trying to say, man?'

'I am saying and saying I know it all. Yes, you are having more than a cousin. You are having a lover. Someone living here in this compound is making love to you and asking and asking what is going on at Pappubhai Chimanlal and Co.'

'Inspector, you must believe me. I've been working for Mr Chimanlal for more than twenty years, and I've never, never told anyone anything about his business. I couldn't, Inspector. I couldn't.'

'You could not' — out with it now — 'because Mr Pappubhai Chimanlal was

165

seducing yourself when you were first becoming his secretary and you have been worshipping ever since.'

Under the flickering tubelight hanging from the ceiling Ivy Cooper's pock-marked face went even paler.

'How — How did — I don't — '

'Madam, never be minding how I was finding out this. It is true, yes? Mr Chimanlal was seducing you, and you were ever since worshipping that man like a god itself. But, madam, what has happened just only a few months back? I will tell you what I am thinking. At last and at last you were meeting some fellow who, for second time only in your life, was speaking soft words to you. You have fallen in love with this fellow. You are no longer loving and loving Chimanlal sahib. You are hating him now for how he was spoiling your life, and you have been taking revenge by getting and egging on an individual by name Yeshwant to steal all the best Chimanlal jewelleries.'

'No. No, no and no. How can you say such things? It isn't true. It isn't. It isn't. Ask anyone round here. Have they seen me with a boy? Ask them. Have they ever seen me with a boy in all the twenty years I've been working for Mr Chimanlal? They'll tell you they haven't. They'll swear it. Swear it in a court of law. Inspector, it isn't true. It isn't true.'

Behind him Ghote suddenly became aware of the big firinghi standing in the flat's doorway blotting out the fine rain. And plainly appalled at this bullying of a defenceless woman.

Well then, he thought, let him ask himself if his Swedish police never question and question a witness till they have gone inside their very head and found whatsoever is in there.

But have I got inside Miss Ivy Cooper's head?

He was beginning to think he had. There was no look of defiance left on the face behind the ruby-red spectacles. So, was there nothing more she needed desperately to hide? To hide from myself? To hide from all the world?

Or was her most private dream still to be broken into?

Yes, he thought, I have not yet done enough. One more knife-plunge is needed. There is one more thing she may be concealing, concealing even from herself.

Plunge in. Plunge deeper.

'Miss Ivy Cooper, very well, you may not have any lover. You may even have been worshipping Mr Pappubhai Chimanlal still.

But what if, at some time, one day or one night, you were seeing the man you are worshipping for twenty years making love to some other woman? Not to his wife, but to some mistress he is having. He was seducing you even when he was just only married, so do you think he has never seduced anyone else? I am thinking you know he has. I am thinking you saw him with some woman. And I am thinking your loyalty to him was vanishing away then like water down a monsoon drain. Yes? Yes?'

'No. Oh, Inspector, if you are thinking that, you just don't know what it is to love a man. To love him and love him, year in, year out. Do you think I don't know he's had mistresses? A man needs a woman. And, even if I'm not the woman he needs now, I can still love him. I can love him better than any woman he goes with for one night, or one week. I can love him more than that barren bitch of a Guju wife he has. I can. I can. And I always will.'

From the doorway there came a choked sound.

'Insp — Ganesh, it's enough. Enough.'

Ghote drew in a deep breath.

Yes, he thought perhaps it is enough. No, it is definitely enough. I am at last believing this poor deluded woman. She has spoken the truth. Under my utmost pressure she has spoken the truth. She told no one, no Yeshwant, no one, about the precious objects that have gone out of those showrooms into the homes Yeshwant has robbed.

'Yes, Axel sahib,' he said. 'It is time to go.'

He turned and followed the bear-like form of the Swede down the slippery wooden steps from the balcony.

At their foot Axel Svensson gave a long sigh.

'I am sorry,' he said, 'but it seems we have not got to Yeshwant here any more than we were getting to him at Pappubhai's show-room. It may be, you know, the end of the road.'

Ghote stood there in the thin rain and let thoughts run through his mind.

Then he in his turn spoke.

'No, Axel, my friend. I am not thinking we have reached end of road. If the long-time loving mistress of one night is not telling Yeshwant what he is needing to know, then there must be one only person who is. Axel, I know now who that must be.'

12

'Dad! Dad! Your dinner's ready.'

Miss Ivy Cooper's voice rang out across the dark, empty compound. But Ghote would not let his companion linger to see if the old man's thick shell had been penetrated by his daughter's strident call. He had too much to say.

'Axel, listen, as we were coming down the stair itself I was thinking. Now all the possible people who could be telling Yeshwant are eliminated. Full stop, yes?'

'But, no, Ganesh, my friend. Listen to me. If Mr Pappu has taken one mistress, isn't it possible, as you were saying, that he has taken more? And to any one of them he may have let slip his secrets.'

For a moment Ghote felt his heart sink. Could this bloody Swede have hit on a whole flood of new possibilities? But then common sense reasserted itself. No. Just think about Pappubhai Chimanlal. He was not a man to go telling secrets to each and every woman he was seizing on to make love to. Far from it.

'Ah, Axel,' he said. 'If you had just only heard Mr Pappubhai Chimanlal telling about

170

his love exploit with Miss Ivy Cooper, you would know that it is to she herself and no other mistress-pistress he is telling his secrets. He is not at all putting all eggs into many baskets. No, he would not tell any of those other women one single thing.'

'Well,' Axel Svensson said, sounding almost apologetic, 'I expect you are right, my friend.'

'Yes. Definitely. So when I had said to myself all possible people have been eliminated and all possible answers have been proved wrong, then I stated whatsoever is remaining, even if it is seeming impossible, must be right. And next, in one flash, I was remembering something, something pointing to that impossible itself. It was just only a few words Mr Pappubhai Chimanlal was saying to me. It was before he was telling why I must not interview Miss Ivy Cooper. What he was saying was this. I am able to remember his six-seven words exactly. He was saying, *She is coming next to my wife*. Axel, to his wife.'

'His wife? His wife? But, Ganesh, are you really trying to say Mr Pappubhai's wife is the one informing Yeshwant? On the strength of those few words alone? And their meaning not at all clear.'

'Well, there is more. A little. Pappubhai Chimanlal was saying also that the wife he was marrying was of a good Gujarati family *in same line*. She was, he was saying, *knowing jewels*. Now, that may be meaning — I am not trying to say more than this. It may be meaning he is sometimes talking with her, not about accounts-this and profit margins-that, but about some particularly fine jewellery he may have sold that day. He is talking, remember, to one who is coming above his long-ago mistress. So I am thinking it is the one and only remaining way, yes? Yes, Axel?'

Axel Svensson stood where he was, thinking.

Then he spoke.

'Yes, Ganesh. Yes, I suppose so. After all, what other explanation is there?'

'Then at least we may try to see if I am right. But not tonight. At this late hour Mr Pappubhai Chimanlal may well be at home, having some dinner or watching television alongside his wife of twenty years. But tomorrow . . . Tomorrow, Axel, he will be all day in his showroom, and she will be at home, all alone except for servants. Tomorrow, Axel, we will go and visit.'

★ ★ ★

Pappubhai Chimanlal's flat at Breach Candy was in a block along a semi-private lane almost at the tip of the promontory known

172

from a hundred years ago and more as Scandal Point. A flat in such a situation, Ghote knew, could well cost as much as would be needed to acquire a small company. The Gujarati jeweller must, with the business knowledge of Miss Ivy Cooper to aid him, have done extraordinarily well.

What would his wife, who had watched him rise up and up in the world, have felt about his success? Would it have been simple pride, despite the mistresses that, according to his secretary, he had felt able to take at his sweet will? Or would the wife have resented such rivals? And at last decided to do what he had thought Miss Ivy Cooper might have done: take revenge. But, if so, who was it she had persuaded actually to steal those expensive objects?

And how had she done that? How could she have even known of a badmash who would at her instruction climb high, high up and get through some open window into whatever flat she had told him held rich loot? And, again, how had she persuaded a man like that to take only the jewelleries she had told him about? What hold could she have over him that had made him leave untouched the silver objects in the glass-fronted cabinet in Mrs Marzban's flat, the gold cigarette-lighter in the Mehtas' filmi drawing room?

Why, when the one lady who, so it appeared, had had sense enough to put her necklace in her safe had foiled him, had he not made good his loss by taking some other small but costly object? And then, another thing even more odd, why was it, if this woman truly was the one directing Yeshwant, that she had put in his way only jewellery that he had to climb and climb to get?

It seemed there was a whole flood of unanswered questions still, even if Mrs Pappubhai Chimanlal was somehow made to confess to having betrayed her husband's secrets.

For a moment, standing at the opening of the lane, a breeze from the sea below bringing a welcome touch of freshness, Ghote thought of consulting Axel Svensson. With his experience in the Swedish Ministry of Justice could he find some answers to the seeming illogicalities that had suddenly now occurred to him?

What a fool I was last night, he thought, to go home and enjoy the quiet company of my wife, with Ved out seeing a film, and not to think at all about where I had got to in tracking down Yeshwant. I should have been thinking and thinking about each and every complication behind the idea that had come to me. And what was I doing? Watching something stupid on television. And liking doing-doing same. Liking not having to think. I was too happy to be mesmerized by those flickering, pointless colours on that fourteen-inch rectangle of glass. I was content and content to be lost with Protima in that silly world, in my *Northern fastness*. Safe.

So, now, now should I discuss all that with this man from winter-cold Sweden? No. No, he is — what? — one visitor from a distant, distant land. And I? I am what? One police detective with my job to be doing.

'Come, Axel,' he said abruptly. 'Let us talk with Mrs Pappubhai Chimanlal.'

The block, Lakshmi Mahal, well named after the goddess of wealth, was more luxurious than any he had visited so far. A Gurkha chowkidar paraded up and down outside. Inside, the liftman wore a distinctly smart khaki uniform with brass buttons on the jacket. Doubly isolated by the lane in which the building stood and by the atmosphere of deadened-down quiet, Lakshmi Mahal's very walls seemed to Ghote to be saying aloud to him, and even to the Swede, *What do you want intruding here?*

Nevertheless, he marched up the flight of broad stairs to the first floor where the Chimanlal apartment lay. Outside its door, however, he could not prevent himself hesitating once again. *Keep out*, it seemed to say. *Keep Out*. It was a massively heavy affair, its solemn polished teak crossed with bands of copper. Between two of these a small peephole door, protected by a black-painted iron grille, stood guard. In the centre, golden letters cut into the teak stated formidably *Pappubhai Chimanlal.*

'Nearly as well guarded as that Shanti house of Mr Amjani's, I would say,' Axel Svensson commented.

'It is Ajmani.'

And we are to go behind Pappubhai Chimanlal's back, Ghote thought, making an effort to ignore his companion. We are seeking to thrust police questions at Pappubhai Chimanlal's wife.

Nevertheless, he raised his hand and firmly pressed the bell-push beside the formidable door.

In a moment the small panel above the golden name opened. A servant's face appeared behind the iron grille.

'To see Mrs Chimanlal,' Ghote said. 'It is Inspector Ghote, Crime Branch, and Mr Axel Svensson, observer from Sweden.'

The little door shut.

They waited.

Ghote wondered if it had been a mistake to tell Pappubhai Chimanlal's wife that the

176

police wanted to ask her questions. If she was guilty of being the person who was controlling Yeshwant — but how could she do that? — she might simply refuse to see them. Or she might take time to think up dozens of explanations of why it seemed she had betrayed her husband's secrets.

They waited outside the heavy door. A minute passed. Another. A third.

What was happening inside? Was Pappubhai Chimanlal's wife even now going down out of the flat by some back way? Or was she standing, desperately contriving how to cover up her wrongdoing? Or telephoning her husband to beg him to come to her rescue? Or telephoning, even, Yeshwant himself?

But at last the big ornate door swung open, and the servant ushered them in. He led them along a wide softly carpeted corridor with at its far end a tall clock in an elaborately carved long case, loudly ticking. Ghote, fighting off the sense of intimidation all the surrounding weighty luxuriousness induced in him, looked almost wildly from side to side. Photographs. Deeply framed photographs, hanging at regular intervals. Some seemed to be of a schoolgirl in sports clothes, perhaps the Chimanlals' daughter. She was posed with various athletic objects, a badminton racket, a hockey stick, once in a swimming costume holding a large silver cup. But most were of Pappubhai Chimanlal with distinguished patrons of his showroom. Was that the Commissioner and his wife? Yes. No. No, thank goodness, not. But there was Mr Anil Ajmani and his wife. And, yes, there was the Minister for Home, Mrs Latika Patel's father-in-law.

Then they were ushered into yet another rich family's drawing room. This one was dominated by a piece of furniture much loved by Gujaratis, a massively ornate swing-seat in dark polished seesun wood hanging from the ceiling, with beside it a gold-shining statue of Lakshmi in a wall shrine. But Ghote had time to take in no more. He was face to face with Mrs Chimanlal.

Herself also very typically Gujarati, he thought, small, neat, well-fleshed body in a quiet green silk sari, its pallu pulled up to cover her head and its colour echoed by the half-dozen plain green bangles on her bare forearms. What he could see of her face was notable for the squarish Gujarati chin and the deep brown, kohl-rimmed eyes. She wore only small gold earrings and her thin gold necklace was half lost in the sari's folds.

'Madam, good morning,' he said.

He paused and licked at his lips.

'Madam, may I introduce Mr Axel

178

Svensson from Sweden. He is studying our Indian police methods, and I — I trust you would not have any objection to his presence.'

'No, Inspector.' Her voice was quietly demure. 'No, Mr Svensson is welcome.'

'Mrs Pappubhai,' Axel Svensson said. 'It is most good of you.'

Mrs Pappubhai, Ghote thought in sudden fury, why cannot the idiot get it right, just once?

But immediately he had to admit to himself that his anger was caused as much by the doubts and dilemmas he felt floating in his own mind as by his Swedish friend's not unreasonable mistake.

Axel Svensson thrust out his hand to be shaken. And, instead of fending off this uncouth foreigner with a hands-folded namaskar, Mrs Chimanlal extended her own hand — it was stubby rather than small and soft — and took his.

'How can I help you, Inspector?' she asked, turning to Ghote with a certain quiet directness. 'You are sure it is not something my husband could tell you? If so, you must go to his showroom. He is all the day there.'

'No. No, madam. No, it is yourself I am wanting to speak with. To — To ask some questions only.'

'Then ask, Inspector,' she said, quietly

smiling. 'I am ready to do what I can to help.'

Was this timid woman guilty of encouraging Yeshwant's daring and discriminating thefts? She hardly sounded like someone able to cow down a climbing badmash.

He felt at a loss for an immediate reply.

But Axel Svensson was not.

'Mrs Pappubhai,' he said, 'can you tell us, please, how it comes about that all the robberies of the man they call Yeshwant are of valuable objects sold by your husband's firm?'

Well, Ghote thought, now it has been said. The challenge issued.

'Inspector,' Mrs Chimanlal said, with what might have been an underlying touch of steel, 'have you come here believing that the person who has been informing this thief Yeshwant is myself only?'

Then, in the half-moment while Ghote was deciding how to take up this counter-challenge, she turned away, quite slowly, and went and sat herself down on the seat of the big looming swing.

'Let me tell you a tale, Mr Svensson,' she said. 'Perhaps as a foreigner you will not know it. It is one every Indian child is told as soon as they begin to beg *Tell me a story, tell me a story*. We call it *The Sparrow and the Crow*.'

'Madam?' Axel Svensson said, plainly puzzled.

Ghote was as puzzled. Not because he did not know the tale. His mother had told it to him almost every night at the time before she had started on the days-long Battle of the Pandavas and the Kauravas. But he could not work out why on earth this woman, who might or might not be the person ordering Yeshwant to climb here and climb there, could want to be telling the tale to Axel Svensson now.

Or is she telling it to myself? And, if she is, why is she?

'It goes, my story, like this,' the demure little woman said as she began gently to swing herself forwards and backwards. 'There was once a sparrow and a crow, and each of them decided to build a nest. The sparrow built hers of wax. But the crow, who was a foolish, thoughtless bird, built hers of dung. Then the monsoons came. The nest made of wax let the rain run off it and came to no harm. But the nest made of dung fell to pieces just as soon as the rains began. So then the crow, her feathers all this way and that, went to the sparrow and cried, *Sister, sister, let me in.* But the sparrow who knew what a noisy, nasty, pushful bird the crow was, replied, *Just wait, just wait, my baby has woken up.* So the crow waited, and got more and more sodden and sad. *Sister, sister, let me in, let me in*, she cawed again. And the sparrow called back, *Wait a minute, wait a minute, I am feeding my baby.* So the crow waited and got wetter and wetter. But at last the sparrow opened her door and let the noisy creature in. *Oh, you poor thing*, she said, and she pointed to her stove, where she had just been making chapattis. *Warm yourself there*, she said. *Warm yourself there.* So the foolish crow hopped up on to the hot, hot stove. And was burnt to death.'

With a single last vigorous backwards and forwards swing she jumped down.

And now Ghote realized why she had told her children's story.

I have been warned, he thought. She may have been telling a firinghi one of our Indian tales. But she was telling myself something more. You noisy, nasty crow, she was saying, I may seem to be no more than a little sparrow but I have a hot, hot stove behind me, a stove not fed with a handful of sticks but with all the wealth and connections my husband has. So do not come poking and pushing into my affairs. Jump back. Turn away.

He drew in a deep breath.

But I am not going to turn away.

13

'Madam,' Ghote said, looking unyieldingly at the story-teller in front of the swing. 'I am sure my friend from Sweden was liking our Indian tale. But, let me remind, we are here on police business. So, madam, I must inform you, I have been making fullest inquiries this past one week and I have to tell you that each and every one of Yeshwant's thefts was of just only one single valuable piece purchased from your husband's showroom. Madam, are you able to account for this?'

He looked at her with all the solemnity of a judge on the bench.

'Why — Why should I be able to account for it, Inspector?'

For one instant there had been a tremor in her voice as she had answered.

Can it be, Ghote thought, can it really be that I am right? Was that story truly directed at myself to warn me away? And has she taken notice now I am not going to be warned? So it is true, is it, that this typical rich Gujarati housewife has somehow — but how? — succeeded in persuading that daring thief Yeshwant to go out stealing? And to steal only jewellery she is telling him about?

He saw there were more questions, many more, that he still had to thrust in.

'Madam, I am thinking it is only yourself who can account for this because my inquiries have shown no one else is able to. Madam, you are knowing Miss Ivy Cooper?'

'Yes, Inspector, my husband's secretary.'

She seemed at this less directly intrusive question to regain the calm she had, by just a flicker, shown she had lost.

He learnt towards her.

Thrust deeper. If she is in cold fact the one who is instructing Yeshwant I must, at any cost, make her admit it. If she is not, then I must be ready to risk whatever penalties may come from insulting the wife of a man of influence like Mr Pappubhai Chimanlal.

'Miss Cooper was at one time, I am sure you are knowing this, your husband's mistress?'

He paused for one instant to see what her reaction was. There was none. He could have sworn to it. So, this was something that over the twenty years and more of her marriage she had come to accept. The docile wife.

'Madam,' he went on, inexorably. 'Miss Cooper for all the years she has worked for your husband has been altogether in love with him. She is knowing also every detail of his business. Yet my inquiries have shown she cannot be the person who is informing Yeshwant where he may steal these rich jewelleries. So, madam, if someone like Miss Cooper, the only person in your husband's showroom fully in his confidence, is not Yeshwant's informant, I must ask again: how do you account for Yeshwant knowing where he can find such fine loot?'

Still he held Pappubhai Chimanlal's wife in his judge's unyielding gaze.

What would she answer now?

But then into the picture he had had of her telling her story as she had sat on the big ornate swing one unnoted tiny detail suddenly rose up.

He saw clearly that the delicately thin gold necklace she wore, just a little more in sight as she had swung back to jump down from the swing and the pallu of her sari had slipped, was formed out of a chain of tiny golden monkeys each one grasping the tail of the one in front of it.

And he had seen just such a necklace —

No. No, I was not seeing it. I was reading about it and seeing it in my mind's eye only. I was reading about it in the report on the theft from Mrs Latika Patel of her sapphire necklace. The sapphire, in a setting of diamonds, was the pendant to a fine, delicately worked, monkeys-linked necklace. Just like what I was seeing a few moments ago.

How many such extremely expensive pieces of jewellery could there be in existence? Was this a pattern Pappubhai Chimanlal and Co. specialized in? Or had Mrs Patel's necklace been, as she had seemed to state, a piece of jewellery made for herself alone? Or, after all, was it possible that, although Pappubhai Chimanlal himself may have assured Mrs Patel her necklace was unique, he had also had made another chain of exactly the same intricate workmanship as a private gift for his wife?

But if the necklace I am now just glimpsing was the only one Pappubhai Chimanlal ever had made, that surely must mean . . .

A wild idea was beginning to flutter like a caged songbird in his mind.

How to find out if it was true?

But Mrs Chimanlal was answering his forcefully thrust-out question, *How do you account for Yeshwant knowing where he can find such fine loot?*

'Inspector, how can I say how such a thief as that goes to work? How can I, a simple housewife brought up knowing very little of the world, answer such a question as that? Right from my days as a girl, I was allowed to know almost nothing. Of course, like most of the girls I was at school with, I had dreams of going out into the wide world. Like most of them I wanted nothing more than to be a doctor, or even an engineer.'

She gave them both a wistful, wry smile.

'But, of course, there was never possibility of that. You know, until I was married I had never even chosen one sari for myself? My mother was saying what each one should be like. And even now I hardly have any choice. My husband tells me I must always dress well, and that comes to mean my saris must be almost the same as the ones I brought to the marriage. No, I know nothing of the world and its ways. Marriage was always my destiny. And, yes, marriage is very nice. There is the security, and to have that is to have a great deal. But sometimes, even now, I think how good it would have been to be a doctor, or a barrister. Many women nowadays are barristers. Or, yes, an engineer. I could be building huge bridges and great dams holding back vast lakes of water from bursting out in floods.'

But Ghote had hardly paid attention to all that. He could think of nothing else now but the glimpse he had had, and still was having, of that fine monkey-chain necklace.

Was it the one Yeshwant stole from Mrs

Latika Patel? Or was it a replica Pappubhai Chimanlal had had made in secret for his wife?

There was only one way to be certain. Somehow to see the pendant that must be dangling just under the top border of her sari. To see if it was, or was not, a rare-rare Sri Lankan, cushion-cut sapphire, worn to ward off Saturn's baleful influence.

But how to do that?

'Madam,' he said, cautiously feeling his way, 'I am well seeing that someone, brought up as you have told, must be knowing little of the world. In fact . . . '

A faint idea had begun to glimmer.

'In fact, madam, what-all you have been telling about your life in a good Gujarati family almost answers the questions I came here to ask.'

Then, as he saw her just visibly relaxing at the possibility that he was after all going to accept the warning in the tale of the sparrow and the crow, the idea took firmer shape in his head.

'Madam,' he went on, scarcely daring to hope the seemingly absurd notion that had come to him could give him his answer, 'I am sure my friend, Mr Svensson, will take back with him to Sweden a fine picture of the good Gujarati home you have here. Madam, I am

188

hoping he will be able, back in ice-cold Sweden, to see in his mind's eye that fine swing itself with you sitting on same telling one of our nicest Indian stories.'

And, as he had hoped, Axel Svensson broke in now.

'Yes, yes, Mrs Pappubhai, a fine life, a fine picture of it. I am only sorry I do not have a camera with me. A photo would be marvellous.'

'But Axel, my friend,' Ghote said, making himself glow with enthusiasm, 'you do not need any camera-whamera now to put into your mind a picture. If Mrs Chimanlal would be so kind as to do it, you can see her now and in your memory ever afterwards, swinging on that swing, back and forwards, back and forwards.'

Pappubhai Chimanlal's wife, relieved of a burden, gave them a sudden almost mischievous look.

'Oh, yes. I would be delighted to do that for you, Mr Svensson. Why not?'

She hopped back on to the swing's broad seat and, with a bigger push than one might have expected from a quiet housewife, launched herself backwards.

Ghote watched, keenly as a hovering kite.

And, as he did so, he realized that the photographs of the athletic schoolgirl he had seen in the corridor outside were not of the Chimanlals' daughter — they had no children, Ivy Cooper had said — but of the woman on the swing herself.

And then the green silk sari slid down by perhaps half an inch more, and Inspector Ghote was able to see what he had planned and contrived to get a sight of: the deep, deep blue of a fine cushion-cut sapphire, set in a surround of tiny diamonds, flashed for one instant into his view. It was only the quickest of glimpses, but what it showed him could not be mistaken.

Mrs Chimanlal jumped lightly down from the swing.

'There, Mr Svensson,' she said. 'Enough for a picture for your mind, I hope.'

'Oh, yes, yes, Mrs Pappubhai. That was superb.'

Then Ghote stepped forward.

'Madam,' he said. 'Madam, now I am knowing. You yourself are the man they are calling as Yeshwant.'

Mrs Pappubhai Chimanlal took one sharp step backwards. The sound of the edge of her sari ripping under her heel came into the big room with all the impact of a pistol shot.

14

Then Ghote knew beyond doubting that his wild idea was right. The pieces fell into place with all the rapidity of some machine designed to slide into correct alignment a score of different odd-shaped segments. Climbing Yeshwant was not a man but a woman. No point now in wondering how an everyday criminal could be daring and discriminating enough to capture those headlines. No need now to ask in perplexity how a rich woman like Mrs Chimanlal could somehow pluck out such a badmash from among the city's criminal population. No need to wonder how a simple Gujarati housewife could possibly control such a wild animal. Plain to see now, too, that someone who in her school days had been a triumphant athlete could manage such dizzying climbs. Even those unusually stubby hands were accounted for. No need any more, either, for that fear that Pinky Dinkarrao would put something in her column which would frighten 'Yeshwant' into losing himself among the millions of India. Scarcely any need now to ask why on earth all the thefts were from places it was necessary to climb up to. And, of course, no need to wonder why they were all of maha expensive pieces from the house of Pappubhai Chimanlal and Co. The puzzle of why 'Yeshwant' had never taken more than one single piece was, too, all but answered now.

'Inspector, it was such fun,' 'Yeshwant' said, stepping clear of the torn edge of her sari, cool and unblushing.

Ghote looked at her. He found that cheerful declaration, despite the inkling he had of her motivation, hard to understand.

'Oh, Inspector,' little, compact, bright-eyed Mrs Chimanlal went on, with the most rueful of smiles. 'You were too clever for me. Too clever altogether. Of course, of course, when I heard you were at the door I shouldn't have taken the risk of putting on Mrs Latika Patel's necklace. But I can't help loving a risk, small or not so small. It comes, you know, from all those long years of being a girl of good family. Never allowed to step beyond the limits chalked out for me. *A girl of good family never walks in the road.* Of course, she must wait for the family car, or at worst she takes a taxi. *A girl of good family never talks to a boy alone.* She waits and waits till she is provided with a husband. So many rules. And all the time I longed to break just one. And, at last, I have. A girl of good family, you know, does not go climbing up the sides of buildings, scrambling in through windows, creeping and creeping past sleeping people and — And just taking away some prized new possession.'

She looked at Ghote now with a grin, rather than a smile, on her once demure face.

'But, madam . . . ' was all that Ghote, suddenly dazzled and bemused, managed to say.

'*But, madam* what, Inspector?'

'Madam, you have been committing crimes. Serious crimes, madam. Breaking and entering is punishable under Indian Penal Code Section 446, *house-breaking by night*. Or, worse, madam, you must be liable under Section 454, *Whoever commits lurking house-breaking . . . and if the offence intended to be committed is theft, the term of imprisonment may be extended to ten years.*'

'Yes. Yes, I suppose I knew that. Or something like it. But . . . but . . . Inspector, you cannot imagine the pleasure it was to be inside those places where I shouldn't have been at all. *Lurking*, as you were saying. But being there, Inspector. Being there secretly in the heart of some person's home, without them having any idea I had penetrated inside. It thrilled me. It thrilled me through and through. It made me feel sick with delight.'

It was as if, now that her secret was out, a dam had burst. The words came pouring through the shattered stonework.

'The first time it was when my husband just said to me one evening that he had sold a pair of diamond karas for a twenty-fifth anniversary present to K. P. Parulkar, the barrister; I suppose he told it because K. P. is such a famous man. He was mentioning also the big, big price he had been paid. And then . . . Then, Inspector, I suddenly saw how I could break out of being the little girl of good family that I still was after nearly twenty years of marriage. I don't know why, but it just came into my head, *I am going to steal those karas*. So I found out where the Parulkars stay. It wasn't difficult. And then I went and looked at that place, and, Inspector, it was so easy to climb up there. At school I was best in class at rope-climbing and all. I felt even the old house itself was saying, *Come up, come up, I am daring you*. And I took that dare. And it was simple, even by night. And then, when I was there inside, I didn't even want to go away with those karas. The pleasure of just being there with them under my hands would have been enough. But — But I had to have something to tell me what I had done. I might have thought afterwards it had all been some dream. I had had so many dreams like that in all the years when I could do nothing. Then, too, each time afterwards I was wanting to tell the world what I had done, what I could do. It became in the end something like one of those drugs that people talk about, the excitement of doing that. And so from time to time I would just ask my husband if he had made any big sale that day. Then I began reading in the papers about what parties and events were coming up so that I could find a good opportunity to go climbing. And that was a strange thing too. Because, that first time I broke the rules I had had to climb up to the Parulkars' flat, each other time I felt I must have some climb to make for Yeshwant, each one more dangerous and daring. Oh, and that was such a nice thing as well, when Pinky Dinkarrao in her column told the story of Shivaji Maharaj and his ghorpad. Suddenly then I became — it was so funny — climbing Yeshwant. Climbing Yeshwant breaking those rules that had made such a cage for me from my girlhood up. Breaking those rules at last.'

'Madam,' Ghote found himself saying, 'I can understand what you are telling. To a certain extent I can understand. I know you were not stealing for the sake of getting hold of valuable objects to sell, like any common thief. But, nevertheless, madam, you were committing an offence, many offences, under Section 446 read with Section 454.'

And now Axel Svensson, beginning to recover from the shock of the revelation, put in his word.

'Mrs Pappubhai, what have you done with all the things you stole? I know about that necklace. Even now it is still round your neck. But the other things? A pearl choker, a very valuable diamond ring, diamond bangles, some — what are they called? — ear-tops . . . Where are they? What have you done with them?'

'Oh, Mr Svensson, they are all safe. Safe here, locked in that wall cupboard we never use, just behind Goddess Lakshmi. Such fine and expensive jewels should be under the guard of wealth-bestowing Lakshmi, yes? And some things I bought at a sports shop to help me in my climbing are there, too. But — But, yes, now that all this is known, I can send each and every piece back to the people I took them from. Yes, I will do that.'

She gave Ghote now a pleading, almost coy look such as might have come from the schoolgirl she had been when she had first built up the muscles that took her climbing eighteen storeys high.

'Inspector, if I send each and every one of

those things back, can't we forget about all this?'

'Certainly not.'

Ghote felt a hot flame of outrage. These rich women, they thought the law did not apply to them.

'Oh, Inspector, this nice Swedish gentleman understands. He knows I wasn't really stealing. He believes me when I say I'm going to return each one of those things.'

'Yes, yes, I do,' the big Swede chimed in.

Idiot. Fool. What is his head made of? Butter only?

'I only wish,' the Gujarati thief went on, 'I had also that diamond necklace Mrs Soonawala was sensible enough to put in her safe before I was climbing up to her flat. I could return that, too. Or, if I had managed to get into Mrs Ajmani's house out at Madh Island and got hold of her triple-string emeralds, she could have had them back also.'

'Muddy Island?' Axel Svensson burst out. 'You were there at Muddy Island? Where the Amjani murder took place? You climbed in there?'

Before Ghote could intervene to point out once more it was *Madh Island* and *Ajmani* Mrs Chimanlal gave a sharp little laugh.

'Oh, no, Mr Svensson. I am sorry to say Mr Anil Ajmani was too good for me with all his security measures. Almost as good as Inspector Ghote here.'

'But you were trying and attempting to steal even from there?' Ghote could not help asking, however much he set aside the blatant attempt to flatter him.

Mrs Chimanlal gave another little laugh.

'Oh, yes, I was trying to get in there, Inspector. You see, I had been reading about that place. It was in the *Pinky Thinking* column. The Ajmanis had given a big party, and Pinky was thinking Mr Ajmani had not held it at Shanti Niwas because some guest might have got to know where were his security lights, or something like that. And then I thought: if I could get to steal that emerald necklace my husband had told me Mr Ajmani had bought for his wife — it was before the terrible murder, you know — that would be the best Yeshwant thing of all. I think, if I had managed that, I might even have been able to stop.'

She gave Ghote another piteous, or perhaps mock-piteous, look.

'But now, I suppose, Yeshwant, poor Yeshwant, must just fade away? No more climbing. No more creeping in the darkness of the night, softly, softly, through someone's home, hearing them in their bed, breathing. And myself hardly making any breathing sounds at all. Oh, Inspector, won't you let me do it once again? Just once? Won't you let me see if I can get into Shanti Niwas after all? I think I could do it, you know.'

Ghote felt a prickle of sharp interest. The Ajmani murder was not his case. But if he could learn how Yeshwant might get into the house, and then tell Mr Kabir how, despite all the security measures, a murderer could break in there . . .

'You are saying,' he asked, 'that it might be possible to get into that place, Shanti Niwas?'

'Oh, yes, Inspector, I am sure I could do it. I failed the first time because they had five-six ugly big dogs going about inside that wall. So then I spent some days looking at the place from a distance to see if anything could be done. I was taking my husband's binocular, you know. The one he bought when he used to go to the races at Mahalaxmi.'

'And you did see how it could be done after all?' Ghote asked.

'Well, it is yes and no. If you are a Number One climber, you could get inside there without too many problems, and the house itself would be quite easy. But the trouble was always those dogs. You could never get past them.'

Ghote experienced a sudden downfall of disappointment.

Very well, he would get something of kudos for having put an end to the famous Yeshwant's exploits. But he had already begun to realize, with a certain grim awareness, that in all probability merely ending Yeshwant's exploits would be all that he would succeed in doing.

The story of the sparrow and the crow came back to his mind. Yes, this sparrow's nest was built of hard, hard wax. Round her she had wound and wound the wealth and influence of Pappubhai Chimanlal, jeweller to all the rich of Bombay. The wretched, feathers-awry cawla that was himself could never truly penetrate her safe nest. Or, if he forced and forced his way in, then the hot chapatti stove would doubtless await him. Daring to stand up against Mr Pappubhai Chimanlal could lead to his being pressured to resign, or to being posted in charge of the Armed Police on the furthest frontier of the state. To anything. Nothing would be heard in public of the ending of Yeshwant's career. Perhaps Pinky Dinkarrao would make something in her column of the mysterious return piece by piece of all Yeshwant's stolen loot. It would be a talking point for a few days, perhaps even a couple of weeks. Then silence.

That would be all. The nest of wax would be untouched.

'So you are saying that no murderer can have got in there?' he asked dully.

'Yes, Inspector, I am. If I could not do it, I cannot see how anyone else could.'

'But they must have done. Ajmani sahib was stabbed to death, and all the Crime Branch inspectors out at Shanti Niwas are certain neither Mrs Ajmani nor the servants could have done it.'

'Well, I suppose, then, there must have been someone there much more clever than poor Yeshwant. With the head of security Mr Ajmani had I could find no way to do it. Except for that man I could easily have bribed one of his guards. I know their sort. I was talking to them even. But none of them could tell me, pay out as I might, how to defeat the double-checked arrangements that man had made. All I was learning was that he himself was one of those iron people who cannot be bribed.'

Easy to see now how Yeshwant was achieving those daring feats if she was ready to go to such lengths, Ghote thought. But, all the same, she must be wrong in her final conclusion. Ajmani sahib had been killed. There, right inside his guarded home. So someone, somehow, must have penetrated into it.

'But, surely, surely, there must have been

201

some way to get in?' he asked once more, unhopeful though he was of hearing any answer.

'No, wait,' Axel Svensson jumped in. 'You must be wrong about that iron man. That security chief himself was bribed. There is always an explanation.'

Mrs Chimanlal looked at him.

'It is not so easy as that, Mr Svensson. Do you think I was not exploring all such matters? Because it is true that the man — he is one Victor Masters, an Anglo-Indian — is the key to that place. He is a devil of efficiency, an ugly hunched fellow marching up and down in his Ajmani uniform, poking and prying, checking and checking again. A devil. I was even able to see such through my husband's binocular. I tell you, you could not find enough money to bribe him if you stole all the jewellery at Pappubhai Chimanlal and Co.'

For a moment the Swede looked as if he believed Mrs Chimanlal thought him capable of such a monster crime. Then he recovered.

'But perhaps someone knew something to the disadvantage of this fellow,' he said. 'Perhaps he was blackmailed into relaxing his guard when he should not have done.'

Damn it, Ghote thought, the Swede is right.

202

'Yes, are you certain,' he asked Mrs Chimanlal, 'that no one could have somehow persuaded this Victor Masters to turn a Nelson's eye at whatsoever time they were wishing to climb in?'

Yeshwant-of-old stood in silence in front of the big swing that had in the end betrayed her.

'Yes?' Ghote said after a little.

'You are right, Inspector,' she said at last, a look of calculation in her dark brown eyes. 'You know, one of the men in his team that I was paying a fat bribe to, although he could not tell me anything of how to get round those security arrangements, did say one thing that might have helped. What he told made me think there may be something not right about Mr Victor Masters.'

'What it is?' Ghote shot out, the thought of how he might put himself once more in Mr Kabir's good books strong in his mind.

His hot question was answered with a cool smile.

'Well, Inspector, what will you give me if I am telling you that?'

'Give you? Give you, madam?'

'Yes, give me. Well, I will tell you what I am wanting to be given. When I was a girl I never dared ask before Diwali for any present that I was wanting and wanting to have. Good girls do not do that. But now, now I have learnt not always to be a girl of good family, I can say what it is I want without shame. So, Inspector, if I am telling you why I believe Victor Masters has a secret, will you be saying no more about your Section this and Section that and all your *lurking house-breakings*?'

Ghote stood half-astonished at this effrontery. Was she really proposing to a police officer that the crimes she had committed would go no further than the four walls of this room? All right, she may have believed that, wife of a man of influence, her crime might eventually be treated with discretion. But now the situation was different. She was making an offer not to the Commissioner for leniency in exchange for influence, but an offer to himself of silence in exchange for information about — About what could very well lead to finding the killer of Anil Ajmani of Ajmani Air-Conditioning.

It was wrong. Wrong.

But — the thought came snake-sliding into his mind — if the information she was offering him led him to the arrest of the man who had stabbed Anil Ajmani to death . . .

So he did not immediately reject the offer.

And that was his mistake. One that Yeshwant-of-old was quick to pounce on.

'I see, Inspector, you are liking my idea. So,

we have a bargain? Yes? No?'

Ghote drew in one long breath.

The Ajmani murder, he thought, solved by myself.

'Madam, yes.'

15

Abruptly Ghote felt as if he had set out walking along a high, high ridge no more than an inch or two wide, with on either side almost vertical slopes running down to far-off spikily piled rocks.

What have I done? What have I said I will do?

And there is a witness also.

He took a quick glance at his Swedish friend. But there seemed to be no look of stern disapproval on his sun-reddened face.

Am I really going to inform nobody, he asked himself then, that Mrs Pappubhai Chimanlal is the daring and discriminating Yeshwant? All right, if I were after all to inform someone, it would be Mr Kabir. And Mr Kabir would inform the Commissioner. And the Commissioner, almost to a certainty, would decide it is a matter where discretion should be exercised, especially when he knows that the criminal has returned all her loot.

So perhaps I am justified — he felt a tiny stab of irony — in doing Commissioner sahib's work for him.

And then — the treacherously narrow ridge seemed to broaden out a little — what I have undertaken to do may result in Anil Ajmani's murderer being brought to justice. And no one in the police will exercise any discretion for that man. Yes, even if I am in the end somehow not getting full kudos for tracking down the killer who first bribed or threatened Victor Masters, security in-charge at Shanti Niwas, to chain up for one hour only his five-six ugly dogs I will feel I was right to get my information from the woman who was Yeshwant.

But what if she is tricking me? What if she has got nothing about Victor Masters to tell me? And, if she has, can I believe what it is she may tell? Or, what if she is thinking she has information worth hearing, and, when she is telling same, it crumbles to dust in my hands?

'Madam,' he made himself say, 'what it is you were learning from this guard you had bribed? What is making you think there is something not right about Victor Masters?'

Would her answer, when it came, be worth having?

'Inspector,' Mrs Chimanlal replied soberly, 'please do not think I am giving you the answer to the Ajmani murder on a gold plate. If it had been easy to discover what is wrong about Victor Masters, I would have found it out and made use of it long before this. But I could not.'

'Very well', Ghote said. 'But tell me what you are thinking you learnt from that guard.'

'All right. It is this. I was asking the fellow what his boss was doing before he came to work for Ajmani Security, and all he could say, rack his brains though he might, was that Victor Masters may have been in the army, or have been in the railways or in the police even. And he was only guessing that because his boss had the habit of always stating the time by the twenty-four-hour clock. Then when I was asking where his boss was staying, it was *Do not know, memsahib, I have seen him get on Churchgate train at Malad Station but where he was getting down I do not know.* I was asking is he married? *Do not know, memsahib.* I was asking did he ever speak of his parents, his children? *Never, memsahib.* I was asking does he go with women? Well, I was myself being the woman of good family when I was talking with him, so I was not putting it just like that. But the answer I was still getting was *Do not know, memsahib.* Oh, and then, of course, I was offering bigger, bigger bribes, and the poor fellow was willing to be bribed. But it was once more *Do not know, memsahib.*'

'But you were not leaving it at that, Yeshwant?' Ghote said.

'For the time being I was. You see, what I would have had to do next was to follow Victor Masters every day when he was leaving Shanti Niwas at the end of his night duties until I could find where he was reaching home. And how could I do that? How could a Gujarati lady who still always goes anywhere in one of her husband's cars follow that man? How even could a Gujarati lady of good family know how to find a detective to do that work for her?'

'But if,' Axel Svensson said puzzledly, breaking a long silence, 'if you were not able to find out anything at all about this Victor fellow, you can have nothing to pass on to us.'

'Ah,' Ghote said, 'but what you have to tell, madam, isn't it, is just that *nothing*? It is meaning to one hundred per cent that there is something altogether mysterious about Mr Victor Masters.'

'Quite right, Inspector. Victor Masters has some secret in his life. He must have. And it is that which Ajmani killer must have somehow got to learn. Would any decent man, with no secret to keep, tell so little about his life?'

She turned to Axel Svensson.

'In India, you know, Mr Svensson,

everybody feels free to ask questions like *You are married? How many children? What is your native place?* They tell me that in the West, and especially in UK, it is considered very impolite to ask such questions. But here we like to show interest in people we meet. We ask, and they answer. No one will hide that they are married, or refuse to say how many children they have.'

Now Ghote felt a lot happier. Yeshwant had had something worth knowing to offer as her side of the bargain. It was not easy to see straight away how he was going to find out more about Victor Masters than the bribed guard had got to know by asking all the questions anyone would feel they had a right to ask. But if there was a secret there, then one way or another he was going to find it out. Then, if it proved to be a secret that Masters would have given a lot to keep, he would have taken the first step. With luck, after that, the simple knowledge of what that secret was would point to whoever had used it to force Masters to suspend for a vital hour Anil Ajmani's famous security arrangements.

'Very well, Yeshwant, if I may be calling you as such for last time,' he said, 'I will tell no one what has been revealed under these four walls, provided of course I am going to learn that certain objects have been returned to their owners. Perhaps, when that is done, you may telephone, without giving a name, to Miss Pinky Dinkarrao. She is certain to put such a nice piece of news, when she has thoroughly checked same, into *Pinky Thinking*. I will wait to see it there.'

* ★ ★

'Well,' Axel Svensson said as they stepped into the lane outside Lakshmi Mahal, 'once more I am inclined to think a promotion must be coming your way, Inspector Ghote.'

'A promotion? No, I am not thinking so.'

'But — But you have found the first good clue to how the Amjani — How the Ajmani murder was committed. It is something not one of your colleagues has succeeded in doing. Yes, he has found the murder weapon, your Inspector Antick. But has that led any further on? No, I think this time — '

Ghote felt he had to stop all this. Yes, he did think very occasionally of what it would be like if somehow promotion came. But it was only in the most secret places of his mind. There were thoughts, he felt, too unthinkable ever to be brought to light. Not even to his wife in their most cherished moments had he murmured *Ganesh V. Ghote, Commissioner of the Bombay Police or Inspector-General Ganesh V. Ghote.* No, not even the least whisper of such things should ever go beyond the privacy of his own head. There even they should be secret, less to be thought of than a dream.

To deflect the blunderingly advancing Swede he seized the nearest weapon to hand.

'Axel sahib, it is Adik,' he almost shouted. 'Adik, not Antick. He is Inspector Adik. Adik, Adik, Adik.'

'Oh, my friend, I am sorry. Sorry. But your Indian names are so difficult for me.'

For a few moments the Swede was silent. Ghote imagined him repeating *Adik, Adik, Adik, Ajmani, Ajmani, Shivaji, Shivaji, Juhu, Juhu, Pappubhai Chimanlal . . . Chimanlal, Chimanlal.*

He hoped that, after this, there would be no more talk of promotions.

'But, my friend, the fact is still there. Ghote is higher in the ratings now than Adik. Much higher.'

Ghote pursed his lips.

'Kindly think,' he snapped out, 'what has Inspector Ghote discovered that is so clever? Yes, he is knowing who is Yeshwant. But he has taken a vow not to tell anyone whatsoever who that is. And, yes, he has some small idea how it may be that the Shanti Niwas killer penetrated the ring of security Ajmani sahib

212

was putting round himself. But what is Inspector Ghote able to do about that? He cannot go to Deputy Commissioner Kabir and tell about this line, because he would first have to say how he was learning what he has. And the name of Mrs Pappubhai Chimanlal is not one that may be pronounced before Mr Kabir or any other officer of the Mumbai Police.'

'Yes,' Axel Svensson said slowly, 'I see all is not as simple as I had thought. So what are you going to do? Are you going to take this Masters fellow in for questioning? I know that your Indian police methods are not exactly what we in the West practise, beatings with lassis — '

'Axel, lassi is a drink, made of curds. It is with lathis, our police weapons, that suspects are, I admit it, sometimes beaten. But how can I get that done, even if I was willing? First I would have to report to Mr Kabir that I had reason to suspect Victor Masters of knowing some good clue to the Anil Ajmani murder, and to do that I would have to tell him about Yeshwant. The thing I am altogether unable to do.'

'Well, yes. Yes, my friend, I see all that now. So what will you do?'

'Whatever it is, I must do it soon. Victor Masters will not be employed out at Shanti

Niwas for many more days, not now that the man all those precautions were made for is already dead.'

'So what can be done?'

Ghote shrugged.

'First of all,' he said, 'I must at least check in police records and also ask army authorities if one Victor Masters was ever in their ranks. Luckily, both keep excellent records. Railway people perhaps not so good. So not much of hope there.'

'Yes, yes. That is excellent, my friend. Something may come of that. In the short times I have been here I have once or twice cursed Indian bureaucracy. But now I must admit there are two sides to that question. But . . . but what if you find nothing? Or if this time bureaucracy is so bureaucratic it provides no immediate answer?'

'Yes,' Ghote said, 'that I am taking into account. So, if I am getting nowhere in that way, I think I must try to penetrate the secret of Victor Masters while Mr Kabir is thinking I am still attempting and trying to find out who is Yeshwant. And to do that I will have to become like one of those private eyes you may see in the cinema hall.'

'But that is good, my friend. That is very good.'

Ghote saw the light of joy abruptly

beaming from his Swedish friend's great big face.

Oh my God, he said to himself, the fellow is thinking he is going to be a Sam Marlowe also, if that is the name of that American fellow.

He thought rapidly.

'Yes,' he said, 'luckily I have had some experiences of what it is I would need to do. You see, the way now to find out this fellow Masters' secret is to follow him whenever he is leaving Shanti Niwas. And in my days I have done plenty of shadowing work, even in disguise. The best thing, you know, is to put on a burqua.'

'A burqua, what is — Oh, it isn't, is it, one of those head-to-foot black garments Arab ladies wear?'

'Yes, yes, it is. Muslim women in India often wear them also. They make excellent disguises.'

For a few paces as they walked along, looking out for the yellow top of a taxi, Axel Svensson was silent.

At last he spoke.

'Some Muslim women must be rather tall?' he suggested.

'Oh, yes. Quite tall, though of course nothing like as tall as yourself, Axel sahib.'

'No. No, I suppose not.'

Very early the next day Ghote, dressed not in an enveloping burqua but in his oldest faded red shirt and plain trousers, was waiting outside Malad Station watching the buses bringing people in from the direction of Madh Island. Neither police records nor Army ones had produced any documentation for a man named Victor Masters. So he had set off from home while it was still dark, leaving Protima and Ved soundly sleeping and the kitchen, like almost every one in the crowded city, full of scuttling night-time cockroaches.

He had few doubts that he would be able to recognize Victor Masters, if only by his Ajmani Security uniform coupled with the short stature and hunched shoulders Yeshwant had spoken of. If the security guard she had bribed had told her the facts, it was certainly Masters' custom after his night on duty to take a train from Malad in the Churchgate direction.

But where would he leave it? Trains out here at this early hour ran three-parts empty. But as they approached Churchgate Station in distant south Bombay they became more and more crowded. Thank goodness, Ghote thought, at this time of day they will not be as jam-packed as at the peak hour when passengers hang out from open doors and are crammed so closely inside that, as they say, no pickpocket has room to dip in his hand. So if I can get into a carriage here next to whichever one Masters enters, I can easily look for him among the few passengers who will get out at Goregaon or at Jogeshwari or Andheri or Vile-Parle or Santa Cruz. Even between Khar Road and Matunga Road not many will leave the train.

But as it gets nearer Churchgate it will not be so easy to spot him. When we get to whatever station he may use nearer the heart of the city, Dadar or Elphinstone Road or Lower Parel or Mahalaxmi or Bombay Central, even as early in the day as this there will be a good many people getting down. If the fellow leaves at any of those, and if he is still wanting to hide himself from any of his colleagues who may be on the train also, he would probably find it easy enough to conceal himself among the passengers hurrying off.

Then, if he is going further than Bombay Central, the next stop, Grant Road, may be very likely. Among all the narrow lanes of the red-light quarter there he may easily have a place where he stays in secret. Or then there is Charni Road and then Marine Lines — he thought for a moment of Punjabi Mrs

Mehta's filmi flat there and the apsara statue on its wall — or finally the fellow may leave at Churchgate itself.

But, provided I am succeeding to spot him if he leaves the train anywhere earlier, even if I am not shadowing him all the way today, tomorrow I can wait for him again. And if I am failing to track him home then, I will wait the next day and the next and the next. But in the end I will learn where this mysterious fellow goes. And then . . .

In the meanwhile, tucked into a recess in the wall of the station building, he watched each bus from the direction of Madh Island setting down passengers. People from there were bound to arrive in batches since they would first have had to take the little ferry across to Versova. With any luck, he reflected, I should be able to say to within six-seven minutes when he will come.

At a tea-stall opposite, the owner was lowering its wooden shutter. He longed to go across and get himself a cup. But he did not dare leave the spot where, hidden, he could take note of every person stepping down from the incoming buses.

Yes, he thought, if I could go across I would give myself the best of those four sorts of tea on that red-painted rates list. I would have a Special in a large cup, never mind it costing twice as much as the cheapest half-cup. Oh, and if in the end I am succeeding in finding out what secret this fellow has, and so get on to whosoever is the murderer of Anil Ajmani, then I would be entitled to a top-class, Taj Mahal Hotel-style treat.

But, at the thought of the Taj, his mind had veered away to his Swedish friend. Irritating though the fellow often was, had it been fair to have said firmly to him that he should amuse himself today by taking a trip to the caves of Elephanta Island? Would the sad man from Sweden find any happiness just only by getting on to one of the little boats at the Gateway among a crowd of everyday tourists and chugging off across the harbour? Well, it was what tourists did . . .

And then he looked up to find he had nearly missed Victor Masters. Instead of arriving by bus, the security in-charge had, in this almost rural area, taken an ekka. It was only when the red plume of its horse's head had caught the bright early morning sunshine that he had seen that the man getting down from it was wearing a uniform. And, yes, he was markedly short in stature and hunched of shoulder.

So, he thought, Victor Masters must sometimes go to the expense of hiring an ekka if other guards from Shanti Niwas are waiting for the bus at Versova. So why, why does he need to keep secret from all the men under him where it is he stays?

Victor Masters, looking straight ahead, started off towards the station entrance at a pace so brisk it was almost a trot.

Ghote pressed himself further back into his nook.

He is coming straight towards me. Has he somehow . . . ?

He flattened himself even harder against the slimy wall behind him.

No, no, he said to himself, I must stop myself thinking about the fellow altogether. If I do not, something may somehow go out from me to him and make him turn and give me one hard look. And then . . . Then he would recognize me again whenever in the next one hour or so I have to get close to him.

No, I must think to one hundred per cent of something else, anything else. But what? What? Try. Try. In seconds only he will be within two-three feet of me.

With all the power of his will he forced himself to think about — About his awkward son. Ved. Ved. Ved. Why is Ved these days so much of trouble? What it is? What? Ah, yes. Yes. It comes down to this: he is wanting more of space for himself. When he was just

220

only a small boy he was not at all minding if we were telling him what he must do, down to his calls of nature. But now . . . now he is resenting whatsoever we are telling him, myself or Protima. Look at the way he will sit in front of the television, even if it is only the advertisements on Zee TV, blotting out every —

He became aware that Victor Masters, face hunched up as much as his body, dark complexion, low forehead, powerful lower jaw skewed markedly to the left, had, directly in front of him, come to a halt fumbling for his wallet.

Ved. Ved. Think about Ved.

And then, wallet shoved back, the man was gone, walking quickly inside the station building.

Ghote, flooded with relief, cautiously went inside in his turn and saw his quarry paying for a ticket.

No travelling *Without Ticket* for him then, he thought. No risking unwanted attention if without ticket he fails to barge through the far-end barrier. He patted himself on the back for having already taken the precaution of buying his own ticket, and one going all the way to the terminus at Churchgate.

He stayed where he was without following his quarry on to the platform. Time enough for that when he heard a train approaching. No point in letting Masters see any more frequently than he need a man in an old red shirt.

At last, judging his moment as the noise of the first incoming train rose to a squealing halt, he went forward.

And, yes, the hunched man was running fast along to the rear of the train to board just in front of the two last *Ladies Only* carriages.

Not so easy at that unoccupied end of the platform to get into the next carriage without becoming conspicuous. Where to go then?

He settled on the carriage two away from his quarry's. It was almost empty and he had no difficulty stationing himself near one of the double-doors, kept open in expectation of the crowds joining later. In that way he could keep watch at each station as they came into it. He would be able to jump off quickly too. Masters, in his anxiety not to give away his destination to any of his men who might have just joined the train, might well leave getting down until the very last second.

So, as they drew into each station in turn, he took good care to lean out and watch the coaches behind. No one left the carriage next to the *Ladies Only* ones at Goregaon. No one left at Jogeshwari, though he thought he saw Masters poke his head out for a moment. But if it was him, when the train began to pull away he had made no attempt to jump out.

At Andheri, where Ghote found he was thinking about Miss Ivy Cooper and her old cantankerous father lost in his world of the loco he had once driven, of the club — what was it? — that he had been secretary of, Masters again looked out. And again, in the end, made no attempt to jump down at the last moment. At Vile-Parle Station Ghote, his stomach rumbling for lack of his usual hot fried breakfast puris, could not help thinking about much-advertised Parle biscuits. Nevertheless, he kept his eye fixed on Masters' carriage. At Santa Cruz and at Khar Road there was no sign at all of his man.

But a good many people had been boarding as they had got nearer the heart of the city, and not only passengers but also the vendors who worked the trains. He had caught sight of a woman with a fluttering bundle of handkerchiefs at Khar Road. At Bandra a man selling gaily painted little wooden flutes had got into the next carriage, and, far along at the front he had caught sight of a bright floating bundle of balloons just vanishing with their vendor. At Matunga Road a little boy, holding in front of himself a round tin of cheap sweets, had joined the passengers who in twos and threes had been entering his own carriage. So when they came to a halt at Bombay Central there were plenty of people pouring out as well as those pouring in.

Ghote strained to watch. But, as the train slowly began to pull away and the hunched man in security guard uniform had still not appeared, he began to worry.

Oh God, fellow must have slipped away this time as soon as train pulled in. And I never saw him. He did. He must have done.

Yes, I was already watching. Or was I? Had my attention slipped for just only one moment? I might easily have missed a fellow as short as Masters. Get down myself now, while I still can? Run along towards station exit? Or . . . ? Or risk staying where I am? Stay here, with the train coming to its last three stops, and no one answering to Masters' description anywhere inside?

But no. No, I must trust myself. I did keep a really good watch-out. I could not have missed him.

Or could I?

Now Grant Road. He leant out once more. If Victor Masters was still on board, this was perhaps the likeliest place of all for him to get off and disappear.

He thought of the fifteen separately numbered Kamathipura Lanes nearby, haunt of prostitutes by the hundred. First-class hiding-place.

Then he felt a tugging at his shirt.

What — ?

He took a quick glance behind.

It was the little vendor of sweets.

'Sahib, want? Cheap, very cheap. Good, good.'

'Go away. Hut jao.'

But still the boy tugged and pleaded.

He turned back with vicious impatience while at the same time trying to crane out further.

'Sahib, buy. Please, red-shirt sahib, buy.'

Again he swung round. He took hold of the thin clutching arm and began tugging at it.

And then, as he had twisted back again, out of the corner of his eye he saw his man. Hurrying away. Uniform jacket over his arm now, but those hunched shoulders under the white singlet he was wearing unmistakable.

The train began to move off. He let the urchin's arm go, and hurled himself out.

In time. Yes, in time.

16

The fiery leap of triumph Ghote had experienced at not letting the wily Victor Masters outwit him died all too soon to ashes. Making his way off the platform, he had risked running up to within ten yards of that short, hunched figure. He had had no difficulty then, further back, in following him as he walked, illegally, across the tracks at the platform's end. A good many other passengers, all presumably without tickets, were making off in the same way and he easily mingled with them.

As he took care not to trip on the rails, he puzzled over the manner in which the security in-charge was choosing to leave the station, since he had seen him at Malad carefully buying his ticket. But, he thought, the fellow must still be wary of any one of the other Ajmani Security guards being on the same train and perhaps following him out of thwarted curiosity.

Yet another sign of how strongly anxious Victor Masters was to conceal anything and everything about his life. And that must mean his secret is something he must at almost any cost keep from prying eyes.

Turning over and over in his mind what the secret could possibly be, Ghote made his way along behind his quarry. Dodging through the early morning crowds — the elderly men setting out to the bazaars with flapping empty shopping bags, the office workers on their way to their jobs clutching black plastic briefcases — he fell as far behind Masters as he had been at any time since the fellow had set off striding out along the straight road ahead.

It was then that the hunt came abruptly to an end.

Losing sight for a moment of the hunched shoulders in the white banian, Ghote had glanced down a narrow lane to take a quick check that the security in-charge had not taken a sudden dive into it. No sign of him. The lane deserted, all but for a pair of scavenging pi-dogs and a few late sleepers lying on their mats outside the narrow-packed, falling-to-pieces houses.

So where was Masters? Nowhere in sight.

Ghote set off at a scrambling, weaving run and managed to gain some ground. But then the pavement ahead cleared and he realized that there was no one in a white singlet anywhere to be seen. And there, a little way ahead, were other lanes to either side. Too many for it to be practical to check each one within a few minutes.

Without any particular hopes he decided, however, to go on as far as the next big crossroads and turn off towards crowded Kamathipura itself and its many tumbled-together houses. After all, it was the most likely place hereabouts for Victor Masters to have somewhere he could sleep during the day with no one to take more than a passing interest in him.

At the hospital near the Jewish Cemetery he turned and, still glancing continually from side to side, made his way into the fifteen Kamathipura Lanes. It was an area that, in its quiet mornings, on the odd occasions he had been there, he had always rather liked. The prostitutes, their night-time activities over, would sleep till late and then come and sit at ease on the charpoys they had dragged out into the daylight, garish make-up left off till evening, chatting, mending clothes, tending their babies, perhaps idly playing some card-game, relaxed and happy. They always seemed unanxious for any business, even resenting as an invasion of their few hours of relaxation the looks cautiously cast at them by the occasional youths walking by. Life went quietly on around them. A goat or two would be rooting about for something to feed on, a tuft of grass, a piece of blown-about newspaper. From a short distance away, where there was a batch of one-man metal workshops, there could faintly be heard the monotonous chinking and clinking of hammers. A scatter of sparrows or of tiny chattering seven-sister birds might be hopping and dodging about.

So, though keeping an eye out for the hunched man in the white banian, Ghote stayed now longer than it was conceivably worthwhile, feeling as he strolled about, at least for a time, content with himself and the world around him.

Then, at last, he had to admit there was really no chance at all now, nor had there been for the past half-hour, of spotting the man who possibly knew the name of the murderer of Anil Ajmani. But he did not feel particularly disheartened. He had done well to have followed the fellow for as long as he had. He knew now, he said to himself, at least to which area Masters went when he had ended his night on duty. He could pick him up again at Grant Road Station next day and with any luck get a little further along the trail. He might even reach its end, find out where Masters stayed, have some solid clue then perhaps as to why the man was so secretive.

On the other hand, he might not.

The problem is, he thought, that it is asking too much to shadow the fellow all on my own. If this was some regular policework, I could have half a dozen constables in plain clothes — one of them even in a burqua — at my command. Even if I had just only one other person with me, we could take it turn and turn about to keep within a few feet of Masters, rather than having to drop back as much as I did when I lost him. But who can I have to help me when I am not truly Inspector Ghote under orders to track down that notorious Yeshwant, but just only one imitation Sam Marlowe?

The Swede? In a burqua, a moving mountain of black cloth, he would attract a mob of street urchins before he had gone a dozen paces. Ridiculous. And almost equally ridiculous to entrust the task to him without a burqua, a tall Westerner doubly conspicuous in an area like Kamathipura. More practical, perhaps, to use one of the minor criminals, under some threat of blackmail, that we often take for this sort of business. Practical, certainly, but now for me impossibly dangerous. That sort of badmash can never be trusted. He would talk about what he had been asked to do and who had asked him, if only by way of boasting. And if he got to know I was working unofficially, he would be the one doing the blackmailing.

And then, as he heard a long ringing laugh coming from one of a group of girls sitting on a charpoy nearby, the idea came to him.

Miss Pinky Dinkarrao, journalist.

*   *   *

Pinky Dinkarrao would be quite suitable for the task, Ghote thought. With the bold coloured saris she so carelessly wrapped round herself and her always wild mass of grey hair, she could go anywhere and be judged as likely as not to be some sort of madwoman. True, Victor Masters would notice her if he happened to look back. But he would never think that someone looking so like a pagalwalli was actually shadowing him. And there could be little doubt that the writer of the *Pinky Thinking* column would jump at what he could tell her was a new move in the Yeshwant investigation. Only when, after some days, her phone would ring and a voice tell her all Yeshwant's loot had been returned would she realize she had been used. And by then, if all went well . . .

But was there a problem?

Pinky Dinkarrao believed she had some right, the right of the journalist, to poke and

231

pry wherever she wanted. And, though Victor Masters was surely fair game, she might succeed in prying further into what was happening than he himself would like. Was he taking in his hand a snake that, grasp it hard behind its head though he might, would yet succeed in wriggling round to sink in its fangs?

But nothing else came to mind. So see Miss Pinky Dinkarrao, put the proposition to her.

He rang her at her office and suggested they should meet 'to discuss something I am not wanting to mention per telephone' at the Badshah Juice Bar. Nearly opposite Crawford Market Headquarters, the rendezvous would surely prevent her thinking what he would ask her was anything other than strictly police business. The thought that she might somehow worm out of him that he was, for the present, Sam Marlowe, private eye, was something he hardly dared contemplate. A headline like *Two Sleuths for the Price of One* or perhaps *Public Servant/Private Eye* in the *Pinky Thinking* column would be such exposure that he could see himself resigning on the spot.

But at least Pinky agreed to the meeting without asking questions. For once. She did, however, insist on an earlier time than he had suggested. And to that he, in his turn, had to agree. He had intended first to go into his cabin at Headquarters and do his best to concoct a report for Mr Kabir that would indicate he was busy hunting down Yeshwant.

If I am not doing that, he said to himself, before long Mr Kabir will be asking what I am doing. And if then it should come out that I am not his Inspector Ghote but just only Sam Marlowe . . .

He had had good reasons for choosing the Badshah, besides its advantages in giving his meeting with Pinky an official air. Its luxury air-conditioned upper room, free like few others in the city of the pervasive ashy smell of cigarettes, was in the afternoons almost always wonderfully quiet. But he was still not altogether happy about going there. A visit to the Badshah had always been a treat for him, though he seldom felt he could go to it at the expense of family commitments. When he did he invariably drank a Ganga-Jamuna, not because its ice-cold mixture of fresh orange juice and fresh lemon was particularly pleasant, although it was delicious enough, but simply because of the idea of it. Somehow its representing the confluence of the mighty Ganges and the holy Jamuna flowing past the all-beautiful Taj Mahal made him see the drink as something set apart. It seemed to be a prize only to be awarded to himself for some triumph he felt he could not openly boast about. But that it was a secret reward was something he kept locked in the deepest recesses of his mind. No one, not wife, not son, and certainly not Miss Pinky Dinkarrao, must ever know what it meant to him.

But today he had felt that the man who had tracked down the elusive Yeshwant was entitled, if ever he was, to that reward. A secret reward for a secret triumph.

However, the moment Pinky Dinkarrao's mass of scarcely combed grey hair rose up from the staircase leading to the Badshah's quiet upper room he was struck as if by a bolt of lightning with the conviction that he was somehow going to have to pay dearly for enlisting her help.

Perhaps he might be able to guard the deepest secret of the Ganga-Jamuna, but something else, he knew, would be wrenched out of him. He felt as if the gauntly angular body mounting up to confront him was Goddess Jamuna herself, rising from the river that bears her name, to protect in all ferocity the baby Krishna being carried across out of reach of wicked King Kansa. But would it be protection Goddess Jamuna was offering to him now? Or destruction?

Hastily he got to his feet behind the narrow

plastic-topped table where he had been sitting waiting, the only customer in the place at this hour, with his Ganga-Jamuna, its glass frosted with cold, in front of him. The table lurched as his thighs pushed against it, and a small splash of the sacred drink tipped out.

An omen, he could not help feeling.

'Miss Pinky,' he said. 'Most good of you to come.'

He saw a white-jacketed bearer timidly arriving in the goddess's wake.

'Please, madam, what can I order for you?'

Pinky took one sharp glance at the glass in front of him.

'Hm,' she said. 'A Ganga-Jamuna, I might have guessed it.'

He waited anxiously to hear what she would ask for. Would this fearful female newshound at once begin to sniff out of him the deep-buried secret of why he had chosen a Ganga-Jamuna?

'No,' Pinky said, however. 'No, I won't have anything. I'll just smoke a cigarette.'

Ghote saw the look of consternation of the face of the bearer at this intended desecration of the non-smoking room. But the man said nothing. Plainly he knew better than to get the Badshah into Miss Pinky Dinkarrao's bad books. An item in

Pinky Thinking denouncing this no-smoking area as a pervertedly strait-laced Western invasion of hard-puffing, pleasure-loving India sprang to Ghote's mind. He saw some such headline as *No Smoking But Much Fire.*

Pinky, crashing down on to the chair opposite him, pulled a battered packet of Charminars from the big leather bag she carried and demanded a light.

'Madam, most sorry. I am not a — That is, I regret I have no matchbox.'

With a heavy sigh Pinky groped in the depths of the battered leather satchel and eventually pulled out a lighter.

'Right,' she said. 'You want some help in putting your hands on my famous Yeshwant. So what exactly are you asking?'

Ghote, though he had prepared his story several times over as he had sat waiting for Pinky, still found himself in a dilemma. How could he disguise as a part of the investigation into the climbing Yeshwant his plan to have Victor Masters followed from Grant Road Station to wherever it was in Kamathipura that he hid himself?

'Madam,' he began cautiously at last, 'for certain reasons it has become necessary to shadow a certain person early tomorrow morning from Grant Road Station to wheresoever he may go.'

'Okay,' Pinky snapped out. 'Three questions. One: what are those certain reasons? Two: who is that certain person? Three: why has the Mumbai Police suddenly become so incapable of undertaking a simple piece of police work that they are having to take the help of a journalist who has better things to do?'

Ghote at once felt as if he were one of his own suspects, marched into the Detection Room and being subjected to an interrogation designed to produce a full confession. Or, he thought with a sudden access of remorse, as if he were Miss Ivy Cooper when he himself had battered at her till she had revealed the deepest secret of her own heart.

He strove to find at least one answer.

'Madam, the police is fully capable, of course, of undertaking any shadow watch whatsoever. But — But in this instance, madam, there are circum — No. No, what it is: is that I am giving you one fine chance to be in at the end of the case. For your column itself.'

'Are you, Inspector? And why should you do that? I don't remember you as being helpful to the press before.'

A thin layer of sweat came up on to Ghote's forehead.

'No. No, I see — Madam, perhaps it is that I am turning over some new leaf.'

'I'm glad to hear it, Inspector. So now read to me what you have found on this newly turned leaf?'

It took Ghote a second or two to unravel the allusion.

'Oh, yes. The leaf of a book. Yes. Very good, very good.'

'And what is written on the leaf, Inspector?'

'Er — Er — Written? Well, yes. Yes. Well, this is written. Yes. It has come to police notice that a certain individual may know who is Yeshwant. But this individual is, for some reasons, unwilling to let any person find out where he stays. So it has become necessary, yes, to shadow him from Grant Road Station.'

Pinky Dinkarrao ground out her cigarette, only half smoked, in the saucer on which his Ganga-Jamuna rested, still untouched.

'All of which, Inspector,' she said, 'raises even more questions than the ones you have so far evaded to answer.'

'It does?'

'It does. So, my friend, why not tell me the simple truth?'

Ghote experienced something of the feeling of hopeless relief he himself had brought to many a criminal at the successful end of an interrogation.

'Very well, madam,' he said. 'I will tell you whole thing.'

'Always the easiest way.'

'But — But I cannot.'

'You cannot? Come, Inspector, try. Just try. Make a clean breast of everything.'

'But, madam, I have taken a vow never to divulge same.'

'But now is the time to break that vow, Inspector. Isn't it? Haven't you already gone too far?'

Ghote thought that probably he had. His conversation with the writer of the *Pinky Thinking* column had not been intended to be on these lines at all. But, on the other hand, he had pledged to little climbing Mrs Chimanlal that Yeshwant's secret would never pass his lips.

He found his lips, indeed, had become drily clamped together. He moistened them. And managed to find some words.

'Madam, I think I may tell you this. After some days you will receive a telephone call. It will inform you that each and every item stolen by Yeshwant has been returned to its owner. You will then, as one excellent journalist, make inquiries of Yeshwant's victims, and you will find that those valuable items have truly been returned.'

'Well, Inspector, now you really are telling me something worth hearing. I won't ask you how you managed all that, nor how big the bribe was that is keeping your mouth shut. Not that I shan't try to find out. But never mind that. Let's get back to the matter in hand. Do I take it, when you said you wanted my help in finding out where a *certain person* stays, that this person may know Yeshwant's true name?'

'No, madam. He does not. Definitely.'

'But that is one of those police lies I hear so much about?'

'Yes, madam. I regret . . . '

'But you still need my help, for some reason that you don't want to tell me, in tracking down this fellow? I take it it is a man, not a woman.'

'Yes, madam.'

She thought for a moment.

'All right, Inspector,' she said, 'now we're on level terms I'll let you off the hook about telling me the ins and outs of it all. At least until you make an arrest at the end of it. If you do. And in that case I demand to be the first to know.'

'Madam, yes. If I am making an arrest, you will learn of it before each and every paper and TV newsroom in entire city.'

Ghote thought then, with a tiny fire of inner joy, that he would never now have to reveal that the daring climbing Yeshwant was not a man but an apparently well-behaved Gujarati wife. And, he added, Pinky has not at all screwed out of me why I am drinking a Ganga-Jamuna.

He snatched up his glass — it was no longer quite as deliciously chilled as it had been — and drained it to the last drop.

17

So early next morning it was Pinky Dinkarrao who was waiting at Grant Road Station, where Ghote himself thought it best not to appear. With the full description of Victor Masters he had given her, uniform jacket, if perhaps only carried, short height, hunched shoulders, face equally hunched together, jaw askew, he had no doubt she would be able to follow him along most of the route he had taken the day before.

Taking the precaution of wearing a different old shirt, and even a different pair of trousers, he had positioned himself at the Novelty Cinema, further along Grant Road, ready to take up the hunt. And almost at the same time to the minute, Masters came into sight, wearing as before a white banian with the uniform jacket on his arm. Some yards behind the easy-to-see figure of Pinky was there. Now, watching Masters from his point of vantage, Ghote saw him halt for a moment and take a quick glance backwards. Without doubt he was making doubly sure he was not being followed.

So, why? Why?

He let his quarry get a little way ahead and then set off in the same direction. All went just as he had expected. Masters turned off to the left, earlier than he himself had done when he had lost him, taking Sukhlaji Street leading straight up to the small district marked on city maps as *Red-Light Area*. For a moment Ghote wondered whether Pinky Dinkarrao would try to come up behind to discover in her turn whatever turned out to be Victor Masters' final destination. But he was hardly worried. Pinky was unlikely to be persistent enough to succeed.

Quietly he followed the steadily progressing white banian as Masters penetrated further and further into the ant heap of Kamathipura. With every step he took, he felt increasingly content. Masters had, all too evidently, decided that any possibility of his being followed no longer existed. He was walking along now with all the air of someone simply coming home at the end of a day's work.

And then at last he swung off abruptly into a passageway hardly keeping apart two rows of wretched houses.

Ghote risked breaking into a run. He reached the galli, so narrow that it lacked even a central drain, just in time to see Masters unfasten the padlock on the thin wooden door of a little cement-walled extension to the back of a building about halfway along. In a moment he had disappeared into it, taking the padlock with him.

There. Tracked down. Here it was at last, the secret hiding-place that this man of secrets had kept hidden from every prying eye. And, surely, that could be only because he had some vital secret to keep to himself.

And soon, soon, though no doubt Masters had locked himself in, he was going to extract from him just what it was he wished to keep from all the world.

Standing at the galli's entrance, Ghote gave a long sigh of pleasure.

So he was not much pleased when Pinky Dinkarrao appeared at his side less than a minute later.

'The door without a padlock?' she asked.

He could not but answer, 'Yes, it is there.'

'So we go in after him,' she said, hardly making a question out of it. 'And, if when we knock he won't answer, you are a big strong man, Inspector, and it would be no problem for you to break that wretched door in half.'

'But I am not going to do it.'

'Not? But I want to ask that ugly fellow two or three little questions.'

Ghote knew she would. And knew, too, that

244

he must not let her. He it was who was going to ask the questions and at last get an answer that would lead him to the killer of thrice-guarded Anil Ajmani. But then another thought came to him. Victor Masters was not exactly a man to cow down before a single police officer. All too clearly, he saw himself lying in the slime of the passageway, with at best a broken nose while Masters disappeared again among the city's millions.

Drawing himself up, he pointed the difficulty out to Pinky.

'So what are you going to do, Inspector?' she said. 'Go away and fetch half a dozen of your biggest uniformed jawans? I am quite ready to keep a tight watch here while you are going.'

But fetching any number of tough jawans was something Sam Marlowe could not do. It was not as if Victor Masters was a murderer. If that had been the situation, he would have had no hesitation in calling on all the forces at his command. But it was not the case. Masters was no more than a frail link to the man who had killed Anil Ajmani in his den at Shanti Niwas. Anything that threatened that link, and the respect that following it up should eventually bring him from Mr Kabir, was not lightly to be thrown away.

So should he leave Pinky keeping her

tight watch while he went and fetched Sam Marlowe's faithful Swedish assistant? Together they should be able to get an answer out of Victor Masters. But bringing the firinghi on to the scene would produce questions by the bucketful from Pinky. *Swedish Police Officer for Mumbai?* he saw her headline.

'No, madam,' he said, 'this is one ticklish business. I am thinking, because I am knowing this fellow has been on his feet all the night, it would be best to let him have a good sleep now. Perhaps if I am coming back later with some trusted fellow officer we would learn who is his friend, Yeshwant, without any of fisticuffs.'

Pinky looked at him. He could see the various considerations going on in her head. *Do I believe this policewalla? Shouldn't I still keep watch on that door? What game is Ghote playing and why, after all, has he taken my help? Or, if I pretend to agree with what he is saying now, will I get more out of him in the end?*

It seemed this last consideration was the winner.

Abruptly Pinky turned away.

'Well, I have a column to write,' she said. 'Just you hope, Inspector, your name doesn't appear in it.'

Ghote's stomach gave a lurch. But then he said to himself that this was an idle joke only, and managed a smile.

'So, madam,' he said, lie for lie, 'shall we meet here itself at, say, two o'clock? The fellow in there is bound to sleep at least till then.'

'Very good, Inspector. And I warn you, do not be late.'

Cheek itself, Ghote thought, coming from the woman who had arrived at the Badshah more than fifteen minutes after the time she herself had insisted on for their meeting. But he let it go. After all, he firmly intended himself to be here again at one o'clock if not earlier. Then, safe from Pinky's prying eyes, he could confront Victor Masters accompanied by his formidably large Swedish friend.

He settled down comfortably to keep his own watch on the sleeping security in-charge, victim of the unknown blackmailer who had plunged the fish knife Inspector Adik had found deep into the heart of protected-protected Anil Ajmani. After a measured thirty minutes by his watch he ventured to creep along the stinking galli and place his ear against the door of Masters' room. Did he detect the sound of snoring? He thought that he did.

He gave it another measured-out thirty minutes and then left to go to Headquarters and, in the privacy of his cabin, make up his report about failing to track down Yeshwant. Already, he said to himself, I have left it later than I should.

★ ★ ★

Half an hour later, coming out into the Headquarters compound with the report in his hand, he could not help congratulating himself on having produced a smokescreen that totally hid the activities of Sam Marlowe, private eye. Then he saw Inspector Adik strolling by, looking every bit as pleased with life as he was himself.

Fellow has solved the Ajmani murder, he thought in sudden dismay. I will never now gain any kudos for finding out the man who was blackmailing Victor Masters into keeping locked up those dogs at Shanti Niwas. No respect from Mr Kabir. Never now any important investigation given to myself.

He hardly dared speak to Adik. But he had to know.

'Adik,' he called out. 'Adik, how are things going, bhai?'

He had never before called Adik *brother*. He had never liked him enough even to think of it. But now, with anxiety quivering through him, the word had slipped out.

Adik turned and came across to him.

'Things going pretty well,' he said. 'I was telling I found the weapon, yes?'

If it is that only, Ghote dared to hope.

'Yes, yes,' he said. 'First-class work.'

'But one big step more today. Just been reporting to Mr Kabir. I have found out how the fellow was getting into that den of Ajmani's. You know, everyone was saying it was impossible. The guru the family has sits in meditation where he can see each and every one going towards that room. And the fellow was altogether firm, that, though he was meditating, he was able to see and take note of anyone passing in front of him.'

'So that is why you were letting off hook all the servants,' Ghote said.

'Yes, that was it. But I have been somewhat too clever for our murderer, I am telling you.'

'How so, bhai?'

That *bhai* again. Will I have to call him as such for ever now?

'I will show you.'

From the pocket of his shirt Adik pulled out a small bundle of photographs.

'Look, you may see it for yourself. I had these photos clicked to make all crystal clear.'

He thrust one of the prints at Ghote.

Blinkingly peering at it in the strong sunlight of the compound, Ghote saw a view of a corridor in a house, Shanti Niwas, he presumed, with right across the end of it, where another corridor apparently ran at right angles, a large teak-wood almirah.

'Now, look at that cupboard,' Adik said. 'What do you notice about it?'

Ghote looked.

'Nothing, bhai,' he said. 'It is an almirah. It is there. But I can see nothing else about it. Unless — '

He thought rapidly.

'Unless the murderer was all the time hiding inside?'

Adik gave a contemptuous laugh.

'With that guru, whose back you can just see at the foot of the picture, looking straight at cupboard's doors?' he said.

'Well, no. No, I suppose that is not the answer.'

'No, it is not. Look again.'

Ghote looked. And thought he had it.

'You are meaning the killer could have slid across that small gap between the top of the almirah and the ceiling?' he said. 'Yes, I should say the guru sitting cross-legged there would not, without lifting up his head by some inches, be able to see the top of the almirah.'

'Yes,' Adik said, not without a tinge of disappointment, 'that was what I was working out. And that is how the murderer got into Ajmani's private room.'

'So it could, after all, be one of the servants?'

'No, no. I have said the servants are in the clear, and so is Mrs Ajmani and everyone else in the house. I tell you, Inspector, we have done our work up there. All checked and cross-checked. The past of each and every servant, even the past of everyone ever employed at Shanti Niwas, right down to a fellow who was Ajmani's PA six years ago. That far we have gone.'

He gave a bark of a laugh.

'It was easy to cross off former PA Mr Vincent Hinks. Job came to an end when he was stabbed to death in some brawl.'

But Ghote took no notice of the casual brutality. Something about the figure at the foot of the photograph had suddenly struck him. Falling all the way down the guru's back were half a dozen rope-like strands of yellowish hair. And he had seen a holy man just like that before.

In the flat of Mrs Latika Patel.

Good heavens, he thought, all the time I was in that flat trying to drag some answers out of that new mother so absorbed in her little daughter, I was not at all realizing that the lady was linked to the house where the Ajmani murder was taking place. She must be Anil Ajmani's daughter, married to that upcoming politician and tea-time tempest maker, Mr R. K. Patel.

Very well, just only one odd coincidence. But what a small world.

And at that moment he became aware that someone was calling his name, in a noticeably commanding way.

He looked all round.

Then he realized the voice was coming from somewhere above him. In fact from the Crime Branch balcony where Deputy Commissioner Kabir had his office, and the man leaning over the balcony wall was none other than Mr Kabir himself.

'Ghote, wake up, there. I am calling to you.'

'Yes, sir. Yes, I am hearing. Sorry, sir.'

'Ghote, I want to know what progress you are making over this so-called Yeshwant business. Come up. Come up.'

Entering Mr Kabir's cabin, Ghote realized that he had in his hand the very report which might have calmed his boss's fears. But he had written it too late, if only by some minutes, and now he must undergo Mr Kabir's direct questioning.

Unless, he thought, my careful account of inquiries I was never actually undertaking may still serve its purpose.

'Sir,' he said, 'in my hand at this moment. I am having my report. Sir, perhaps if you were reading same it would save time.'

He placed the sheets down among the handful of silver-shining initialled paper-weights on the big semicircular desk.

The Deputy Commissioner took them up, frowned slightly at a certain messiness.

Ghote turned to go.

'Stay,' Mr Kabir barked.

He read in silence while Ghote waited, standing at rigid attention.

'Inspector,' Mr Kabir said at last, his out-Britishing the British accent more to the fore than ever, 'this tells me precisely nothing. So far as I can see all you have been doing since I entrusted you with this very important inquiry is to go trailing round duplicating work other officers have done before you. And you've taken your time about it, too. What have you been doing in the past two days? Missing out on everyone you ought to have been questioning. That's what. It won't do, Ghote. It won't do.'

'No, sir.'

'Then let me make this clear. Unless in another forty-eight hours you can come to me with definite progress, preferably to say you've put the handcuffs on our discriminating Raffles, then I shall take you off the case. And very probably I shall find some less onerous duties for you in some other branch of the service.'

Ghote thought for one moment of saying, flat out, that he had in fact forced Yeshwant to finish with thieving, and that the climbing thief was not a man but a Gujarati lady of good family with an influential husband. But he knew he could not do that. His promise was his promise.

'Yes, sir,' he said.

He clicked heels and left.

* * *

In something of a panic — forty-eight hours only to get Victor Masters' secret out of him — Ghote hurried to collect his towering Swedish frightener at the Taj. And found his plans once again disrupted. At his ring at the bell Axel Svensson opened the door of his room, but it was plain he had risen from bed to do so, white-faced.

Stomach troubles, Ghote instantly diagnosed. Bad stomach troubles.

But it was worse.

'Axel, my friend,' he ventured. 'You are not

looking very much well.'

'Oh, Ganesh, Ganesh. A terrible, terrible thing happened to me.'

Another terrible thing, Ghote thought, his concern evaporating like a splash of water under the midday sun.

'What it is?' he enquired, trying to sound decently anxious.

'I know that you suggested I ought to take the trip out to Elephants Island — '

'It is not Elephants. It is Elephanta.'

'Yes, yes. But yesterday I didn't go. I was feeling rather miserable, and I stayed here in the hotel all day.'

Ghote felt a small dagger-twist of remorse.

Did I truly say it so firmly as that? Did I say *ought to*? That was hardly making just only a passing suggestion so as to get him off my head.

'Go on,' he said warily.

'Yes. Well, I did mean to go on the trip today. I really did. But then I decided I would first have one more walk about the city. I know I got into trouble doing that before. Twice. But I thought, if I kept my eyes wide open, I should be safe this time.'

'But you were not?'

'Yes. Yes, I'm afraid I was not. And, oh, it was horrible, Ganesh. Horrible.'

'But you are not telling what it was,' Ghote demanded, thinking, *I need this man, I need him now.*

'No. No, you see, I hardly like to speak of it still. But — But I was strolling along Mahatma Gandhi Road — M. G. Road, is that what it's called?'

'Yes, yes.'

'And at the far end I stopped to watch one of those games of cricket on the OL Maidan.'

'It is Oval.'

'Oh, is it? Well, although I have spent some time in England, I have never been able to work out how you play cricket, and I thought that this time I would crack it. Yes.'

Ghote remembered himself then, staring unseeingly at that earlier game on the Oval Maidan when a voice trumpeting, *It is Mr Ghote? Inspector Ghote?* had broken into his happy reverie, and all the disasters and complications that had arisen from that moment on.

'Yes, you were watching some cricket?' he prompted sharply.

'Yes, yes. And a man came up and stood beside me. After a while he told me this was a festival day and asked if I would like to see a typical Hindu religious ceremony. Of course, I said I would. Something so colourful would be very interesting to me.'

That is what he is calling keeping open his eyes. Falling for just only the same trick he was falling for when that idler caught him and told him that nonsense story about the man having his kidney stolen.

'So . . . ?'

'So he was leading me some little way, in the direction of the sea I think, and then he was taking me through some big gates. There was a sign above them, but it was in Indian writing. So I asked where this was. At first he didn't reply. But when we were quite far inside, *This is the Burning Ghats*, he said. The cremation grounds, I asked. *Yes, yes.* Well, I was not too sure I wanted to go into such a place, but we were there and I thought he had been kind to go so far with me. So I stayed with him.'

'Yes,' Ghote said, gritting his teeth, 'we have had complaints from tourists about badmashes at the Burning Ghats before. They are taking tourists in there, going to some quiet corner and demanding money, with threat from knives also.'

'Oh,' said Axel Svensson.

'But that was not what was happening to you?'

'No, no. In a way, perhaps, it was worse.'

'What of worse?'

'Well, after a while this man was suddenly

seizing my arm and saying, *Come over here, over here*. I went, though already I was beginning to feel quite uneasy. He made me join a little group, half a dozen people, standing round something. Soon he pushed me right to the front and I saw a deep hole had been dug there, like a shaft going downwards. And at the bottom of it there was — There was something, covered in flowers. Then, *Look, look*, that man said, *they are burying a baby. You know, if a child dies before it has reached the age of nine months the body is not burnt but buried. It is our custom.* I realized then that the people standing round were the child's family, or rather the father and uncles, perhaps. There were no women there. Then I saw the slow tears that were trickling down the father's face. And there I was, being made to intrude on his grief. I tell you, Ganesh, I felt as bad as if I was committing rape. I — I took out my wallet. I thrust at the man all the notes I had, and ran out of the place. I saw a taxi. I jumped in. Luckily I found I had just one more fifty-rupee note when I got here. And then I came up to my room, and fell on to the bed.'

Ghote looked at the Swede. Now when he really needed him it seemed he would not be able to leave his room. It was plain he had been deeply disturbed, and, yes, rightly so. One foul trick to play on an innocent Westerner. He ought to be left to see what sleep could do.

But there is no one else to come with me to where Victor Masters is lying asleep. And I must, I must, wake him and question. I must break into the hidden places of his mind and find out what is the secret he so much wants to keep. And then . . . then ask that key question: *Who was it, when he also had found your secret out, who made you silence the dogs at Shanti Niwas?*

And I cannot ask that without back-up. Victor Masters, it is plain, is tough as any goonda in the slums. He will have no intention of letting his secret, whatever it is, come to light. All right, pull him into the Detention Room somewhere and keep him there all day and half the night with nothing to eat and nothing to drink, and the answer would come out soon enough.

But now, at the very least, a man who looks as if he can use his fists is needed. And for Sam Marlowe no one but Axel Svensson is available.

Yet, looking at the Swede, back sitting slumped now on the side of the big bed, he thought it was doubtful if he could get him even as far as Kamathipura. So how threatening would he look if Victor Masters started making a fight of it?

But time is getting short. I must be back there by one p.m. I must. So, try. At least try.

'Axel, my friend, I am not at all liking to ask you this. But you have said you very much wish fully to go back to those days when, as official observer, you were so much of help to me.'

At these words the Swede's big head did rise up a little.

'Axel, let me tell you how things have been going since we left Mrs Pappubhai Chimanlal. I have succeeded to find, with somewhat of help from Miss Pinky Dinkarrao, where it is Victor Masters hides. It is in a room in Kamathipura red-light area. But I was feeling it would be one hundred per cent idiotic to tackle such a brute of a man with only a lady beside me. So I was leaving him there, hopefully still sleeping after his night on duty.'

He had been avoiding looking directly at the Swede as he had spoken. But now he took a glance at him.

He was sitting up straight on the bed.

One quick look at his watch. Not far short of one o'clock before we get to Kamathipura, even if I persuade him on to his feet this moment.

Risk everything.

'Axel, will you come with me there now? I am needing somewhat of support.'

The big firinghi stood up, went like a leaden-legged giant towards the door.

But it turned out that Ghote's troubles were not over yet.

'Wait,' Axel Svensson said as the lift doors opened on to the hotel lobby.

'Yes, yes? What it is?'

'Money, my friend. I was telling you, I spent every last rupee I had getting back here by taxi. I cannot come out without getting some more. It will take only a few minutes.'

'But, Axel, I have money. If you need any I can let you have something.'

'No, no, my friend. In a strange country I do not dare go about without a full wallet. I would not feel safe.'

Ghote thought of arguing. All right, money in one's pocket was like a riot shield if some unexpected assault happened, whether physical or an attack on one's peace of mind. But it was not everything.

Yet one look at the fixed expression on the Swede's face and he realized it would be quicker not to argue.

Only, the *few minutes* the Swede had said it would take to cash a traveller's cheque were in the end a good deal longer than that. He had failed to reckon with the coils of bureaucracy.

So when they got out of their taxi in Sukhlaji Street, it was already several minutes after one o'clock. Heartlessly, Ghote took the still pale-faced Swede at a run towards the narrow slime-running galli in which Victor Masters' cement-walled refuge lay. Yes, the firinghi had had a mentally exhausting morning. But, if Masters was one of those people who needed very little sleep, he might wake up at any moment.

They reached the galli entrance. Ghote swung round to look into it.

And saw Pinky Dinkarrao sitting slumped in the inch-deep filth, her face as pale as the Swede's had been.

The wooden door of the room where they had left Victor Masters was swinging back on its hinges.

18

'Madam,' Ghote called to Pinky Dinkarrao, 'what has happened?'

But he knew in an instant. The curiosity-consumed journalist had, of course, attempted to steal a march on him and had come back to Masters' refuge early. Although he had himself attempted to get back to Masters an hour before Pinky, he still felt furious. He should have known. He should have damn well known. But somehow he had never been able to believe the extent to which anyone with a journalist's prying itch would go in order to learn a secret.

He turned now to Axel Svensson, standing gaping beside him.

'Do not mess your shoes, and your trousers also,' he said, 'by coming into this galli. Go back down to Sukhlaji Street and find a taxi. Miss Dinkarrao will need same.'

Then he plunged into the galli, telling himself he had in his day been in yet filthier places. In a few strides he reached Pinky Dinkarrao and pulled her, tear-stained, to her feet.

'If you were being fool enough to leave the field open,' she said, 'I was not going to be so fair-play as to wait till you had got your answers before asking that devil my questions.'

'Very well. But what answers were you getting?'

She laughed.

'A filthy wet behind, Inspector. That was all the answer I got. And I hope it pleases you.'

'Well, I must consider you were paid out for your journalist's trick. But tell me exactly what was happening.'

He did not expect to learn anything that would retrieve the situation. But he felt he must at least try.

'What happened? Well, your fellow was not as much of a sleeper as you thought. By the time I had got here he had already packed up all his belongings and had an old scavenger woman clearing out everything left in the place.'

That came to Ghote as another blow. Had Masters taken flight because he had seen that he was being shadowed? Had he given the fellow warning? But no. No, he had not been seen. He had been, if anything, too cautious in trailing him. That was why he had lost him yesterday. And earlier this morning, when he had been using Pinky, even less could

Masters have suspected anything. So why then had he decided to leave the room he had been so anxious not to let anyone know about? No answer came to mind. But it was something to think about. Definitely.

He turned and looked in at the room.

It had been stripped down right to its flaking lime-washed walls. Everything that had ever been in it had been taken away with all the thoroughness of an invading horde cleansing a newly conquered territory.

He stepped inside and gave those walls a thorough inspection. People wrote things on walls, telephone numbers, addresses, reminders. Victor Masters had written nothing. At every point all that came up was, once more, secrecy. Secrecy, secrecy, secrecy.

He went back to Pinky, now standing at the end of the galli trying both not to touch any contaminated part of her soaked sari and to wring out of it every trace of the galli's slime.

'Madam,' he said, 'we would put you in a taxi in two-three minutes only. But first finish telling what happened. There may be some clue there.'

'No, there won't. It was all over too soon.'

She gave a wry smile.

'The fact is that it was my fault from the very beginning,' she went on. 'I was not going to tell you this. But yesterday before I saw you I had some not very nice visitors to my office. They were what made me late coming to the Badshah, gentlemen very firmly pointing out that what I was writing about Yeshwant was, to their minds, insulting Shivaji Maharaj. I imagine you know where they came from.'

'I am able to guess.'

'Well, to tell you the truth, I don't like even to take their name. But, yes, it was those fundos coming invading into my little private place where Pinky thinks. And under open threat of force — yes, force — there was nothing I could do about them. I had to promise that Yeshwant would not appear in my column again. But, when in the Badshah you told me someone would ring and say all Yeshwant's loot had been returned, then I thought I might write one last piece about him. And perhaps at the same time I could say something about that invasion of my territory. A *Yeshwant Retires* story would bring me so much kudos I could afford to defy those people. And so I was doubly pleased to fall in with your shadowing plan.'

'To trick me and come back, yes?'

'Yes. And that is why I've got a ruined sari and a very unpleasant wet feeling all the way up my legs. The moment that ugly fellow of yours saw me he seized hold of me by the shoulders, shook me like a rat and flung me down where you found me. I think even I passed out altogether. All I can remember is seeing that swine walking away, with some sort of knapsack on his hunched back.'

'Madam, I am sorry. But tell me, what like did that scavenger woman look?'

'Like all such women, for heaven's sake,' Pinky replied irritatedly.

'But were you seeing which way she was going?'

'No, I was not. I was looking at that ugly, twisted face thrust into mine and wishing I was somewhere else, anywhere else.'

'So she had finished her work in that room?'

'Yes, yes, I suppose she had. She was going away when I came, with a big gunny sack over her shoulder. And no baksheesh from Mr Ugly. He was too busy shaking me to death.'

With that, he escorted the soaking and smelly journalist to Sukhlaji Street where, he was thankful to see, Axel Svensson there with a taxi. Together they put the stinking writer of *Pinky Thinking* into it and saw her off, Ghote not daring to imagine what Pinky was thinking as she went.

*   *   *

It took him the rest of the morning and a good part of the afternoon to locate the scavenger Pinky had declined to give any description of. But going tirelessly round the area, questioning every old woman he came across, with Axel Svensson plodding along at his elbow offering helpful but unhelpful suggestions and the words *forty-eight hours* never quite out of his mind, find her eventually he did. She was a little wizened creature, scanty white hair screwed into a bun at her neck, dust-impregnated bright red sari tight-drawn between her legs, rubber chappals on her tiny feet.

'Sister, was it you who cleared a room for a man with a twisted jaw this morning?' he asked

'Perhaps . . . '

Ah. At last.

'Sister, this firinghi will give you much money if he can see what you were finding there.'

He wondered whether to tell the Swede what he had promised, in Marathi, he would do with some of the cash eventually exchanged against a traveller's cheque. And decided not to bother.

The old scavenger looked Axel Svensson up and down, and eventually seemed to decide he was fool enough to do what Ghote had promised.

'Come,' she said.

They followed her to one of the houses in Kamathipura Fifth Lane where she was mistress of a few sacks of rubbish waiting in a corner to be sorted, as bottles to be refilled, or as rags or paper for the rag-merchant or the paper factory or, finally, as broken glass, eventually to be made into new bottles.

The old woman, scarcely half Axel Svensson's height, boldly faced up to him.

'Money,' she said in English.

Rapidly Ghote explained what he had promised her. Coin by coin the Swede counted out the sum from the copious handful of change he had got from the taxi-walla he had found to take Pinky Dinkarrao home. At last the sack the old woman had carried away from Victor Masters' swept-clear room was tipped out in front of them.

Its contents formed a not very hopeful pile. Besides a tattered plastic rug, which Victor Masters must have used to sleep on, a chipped tin plate and a steel glass there was little else but a clutter of banana peels, scraps of paper and old cartons evidently discarded over some weeks past.

'All the same, we will have to examine,'

Ghote said. 'Each and every thing. It is the only chance we are having of finding a clue.'

Lumberingly Axel Svensson got down on to his knees.

'Axel sahib, you are being a tip-top detective now,' Ghote said. 'I am happy to be taking your help. Kindly look first for any piece-paper with handwriting on. We may be lucky.'

They were not. It took them a good deal of time to sort through every item in the sack. But in the end they had come across not a single handwritten word.

'That also is significant,' Ghote told the Swede as the big man gruntingly got to his feet again. 'You see, Victor Masters has gone to very, very great lengths to obliterate each and every clue that may link him to anything from his former life. But he must have had such a life. Someone somewhere must be sending him, for instance, letters, even if only some government department. No one, except the poorest of the poors, can escape such. So that man has a secret. He has. And I am going somehow to find it out.'

He looked at the few things of any value that Masters had seemed willing to have left behind, the chipped tin plate, the steel glass and a small knife. Idly turning over this last, beneath the layer of sweat stains on its wooden handle he saw something.

'This also was in the room?' he asked the little old scavenger.

'You are calling me one liar?'

Eyes glittered. A battle in prospect.

'No, no,' Ghote quickly soothed her. 'It was only, I was thinking, the single thing worth having in whole pile.'

'And you are not having. Not unless you pay-pay.'

'Well, I will give you even two rupees for it.'

'Four.'

'Three.'

'Now?'

Ghote thrust his hand into his pocket, brought out three coins, passed them over.

'You are wanting glass also? It is good. Three rupees only.'

Ghote shook his head.

'Two? Two? Two rupees for this glass, like new. Like new.'

Waving her off, Ghote led Axel Svensson away.

'But why were you buying that knife?' the Swede asked when they were barely out of the old bargainer's hearing. 'It wasn't any good.'

Ghote smiled.

'Look,' he said.

He held the knife up so that the Swede

271

could see its handle. On it in smudgily stamped, small blue Devanagari-script letters were a couple of printed lines.

'It is the address of a shop down in Colaba,' he told the Swede. 'It must be the sort of place selling anything that poor people, like the Koli families down there, may be wanting.'

'Koli families? What are they?'

'They are, if you like, the people to whom Mumbai itself should be belonging,' he answered with a little smile.

'But — '

'Yes, you see, they are descendants of the fisherfolk who were here when all this city was just only a few islands, mostly at times covered by the sea itself. And ever since then, when the Portuguese were coming and afterwards the British, they have stayed where they were. In all those years the city has let their little villages remain, like a grit in an oyster, you know.'

'And have they become a pearl?'

Ghote laughed.

'No, no, not at all. They are barely making living from fishing, and some small-time smuggling also. But this knife may turn out to be a pearl, gritty though it is seeming. If Victor Masters was buying this knife — dirty, you see, but the blade not at all old — the people at this shop may know something of him. So, chalo.'

'Chalo? What is that?'

'It is *let's go*. Let's go, Axel, my friend. And let's also hope we would be lucky.'

★   ★   ★

They were lucky, and they were unlucky. Ghote had no difficulty in finding the shop. It was a ramshackle place, half permanent, half under a low roof, not far from the wharf where the boats of the Koli community were tied up after their dawn fishing. They saw, as they had approached from the slightly higher ground where the tall blocks at Cuffe Parade rose into the sky, that its roof in fact was chiefly formed out of a huge old discarded film hoarding. The monstrously enlarged painted face of the heroine stared up at them, together with part of the film's title in English script, *Chor*.

'Chor?' Axel Svensson asked. 'What is that?'

'Thief. It is meaning *thief*,' Ghote answered, thinking to himself that though he had tracked down the thief Yeshwant he still had far to go to find the murderer of Anil Ajmani. And much less now than forty-eight hours to do it in.

Leaving the Swede, he plunged into the shop. At once the dark of the interior after the brightness of the afternoon sun brought him to a halt. He stood where he was, blinking and shaking his head.

Then, before he could open his mouth to ask a cautious question about who had bought the little knife, he heard a voice from the inner depths, growling rather than speaking.

'Policia. Damn policewalla.'

Ghote was all too familiar with the way the city's goondas could recognize him as a policewalla at a glance. It must be, he had thought long ago, something about the way he unconsciously stood, or the look on his face when on duty, which he could wipe from his features only with a deliberate effort.

But nevertheless he cursed himself for having stepped into the shop without making more of a careful assessment. No doubt it must be a place engaged, as he had mentioned to Axel Svensson, in small-time smuggling.

But there was no help for it now.

'Police, yes,' he snapped out, as the shopkeeper who, looking much like a Koli himself, gradually came into his view as he became accustomed to the interior darkness. 'And questions I have to ask.'

Then, still a little bemused in the dim light, he saw the fellow was advancing towards him. And in his hand now, seized from among half a dozen objects fastened to the wall at his back, was a fish knife, its fearsomely sharp blade glinting.

'One question,' the man growled, 'and I will throw you out like a rotten onion.'

19

Ghote retreated. It was not something he liked doing. But he saw no other way open to him. He had made the mistake of stepping from bright sunlight into this dark shop without pausing to discover who might be there inside. He must pay for that.

For a brief moment he had considered calling in Axel Svensson. The sight of the big Swede might have been enough to make the knife-wielding shopkeeper think again. But on the other hand it might not. The Swede coming blundering in, blinking and peering in the semi-darkness, would not have looked all that menacing. Nor was there any reason to involve him in any trouble.

So, it is what they are calling better part of valour, he had said to himself. And had backed out of the place.

'Axel, my friend,' he said, as he emerged, 'I am having second thought about asking questions here just now.'

He looked up and down the lane where the shop stood halfway between the hanging fishing nets at the wharf and the road beyond with its occasional passing cars.

'Yes,' he said, 'I see an Irani restaurant up there. We'll go and sit inside until I am seeing come out the fellow who owns this shop, one top-notch ne'er-do-well.'

'But what is an Irani restaurant?' Axel Svensson asked.

If only all the questions I have to answer were as easy, Ghote thought.

'Irani restaurants,' he said, 'are to be found all over the city. They are run by Parsis of the poorer kind and have been inherited down the years from their forefathers itself coming from Persia or, as they are now saying, Iran. They give you decent food at decent prices, if not at all posh.'

Axel Svensson gave a tremendous grin.

'Then challing,' he said. 'No. No, wait. No, that's not right. It is . . . It is . . .'

'Chalo?' Ghote suggested eventually.

'Yes, yes. Chalo. Let's go.'

The restaurant was much like the scores of its kind Ghote had had occasion to use since he had first come to Bombay. Outside it there was a blackboard with a long list of things its patrons were asked not to do. *No smoking. No fighting. No talking loud. No discussing gambling. No spitting. No combing. No sitting long. No division of beverages. No water to outsiders.*

'Not too welcoming,' Axel Svensson said.

'Well, look, that list is headed by word *Sorry*. And this area is full of people who would be taking advantages. The owner must earn his living after all.'

'Yes, yes.'

Inside, Ghote chose the nearest marble-topped table to the window, despite the fact that it was leaning heavily to one side on its one ironwork leg. He pulled out the tin-seated chair which would give him the best view of the shop under the *Chor* awning.

Axel Svensson was looking round.

'Those cakes on display,' he said. 'The yellow and pink iced ones, I have to say that they are attracting a lot of flies.'

At that moment the proprietor, who looked as if he was permanently armed with a fly-swat, brought it down on the dark wood surface of the counter in front of him with a whack that belied the frail appearance his loose white shirt and pyjamas gave him.

Ghote felt he could hardly brush aside the Swede's complaint.

'Yes, there must be flies,' he said. 'You must expect flies when, even up here, you can smell the little fish they are drying by the hundreds on wooden racks down there. What is being called Bombay duck. But, if you are too worried, have just only a cup of tea.'

The proprietor, victory over one fly

278

achieved, came up to take their orders.

'I am always happy to see a police coming in,' he said. 'Then I am knowing nothing will spoil my calm.'

Axel Svensson looked up at him.

'Do you know my friend?' he asked.

'No, no, sahib. But you can always tell the police.'

Ghote, sighing, ordered the Swede's tea and an omelette for himself.

He had eventually eaten a second omelette, thinking of the hours out of a total of forty-eight ticking away. Then he had scraped the fly-spots from more than a few pink iced cakes. At last, with the first signs of the swiftly coming dark in the sky, the owner of the film-hoarding shop suddenly emerged and began to walk briskly away in the direction of the wharf.

Ghote, tugging an overgenerous fifty-rupee note from his wallet and slamming it on to the leaning table, was out of the door at a run. Scarcely looking to see if Axel Svensson was following — he would welcome the back-up the tall firinghi might seem to provide — he pelted down the lane ahead.

In a minute or two he had overtaken the quickly walking shop-owner. He whirled round and confronted him head to head.

'I had questions,' he banged out. 'Inspector

Ghote, Crime Branch.'

A look of thwarted rage came up on the fellow's dark face. His hand went down towards the top of the red lunghi round his waist, his sole garment.

But Ghote was quicker.

He darted forward, seized the top of the knife-hilt he had seen and flicked the weapon out into his own hand.

Right, he said to himself. I am not going to let this badmash go on in his comfortable lying life. I will thrust my way inside his head until I am getting to truth, even if I have to thrust this knife into him here and there to make him know I mean business.

He flipped the knife round and put its tip against the man's bare chest just under his windpipe.

'Now,' he said. 'No nonsense. A man was coming into your shop not long ago, a man with hunched shoulders and a jaw that is always twisted to the left.'

'No. No. No, I have never seen.'

But it was all too obvious from the momentarily upturned whites of his eyes that the fellow had, indeed, seen Victor Masters.

'Yes,' Ghote said.

'No. Nev — '

Unhesitatingly, Ghote pushed the knife he was holding a quarter of an inch forward. He felt the flesh at the top of the liar's chest give a little, and knew that, if he were fool enough to look down, he would see a trickle of bright blood there.

'You know that man,' he said, stating the bare fact.

'Inspector, once-twice . . . once-twice I may have seen.'

'Not once-twice,' Ghote shot back. 'More.'

He decided to take a risk.

'You are knowing him well,' he said. 'He is coming to your shop many times, to buy food and drink. A plate, a steel glass and a small knife for cutting food also.'

He saw he had hit on the facts.

'So what is his name?' he demanded.

'Inspector, he never said it. I promise you that. Never. Ever.'

Ghote guessed he was telling the truth now, at least about Masters' name. He took one more risk.

'Very well. But he was telling you, just two-three days back, he was going away, yes?'

He watched the face in front of him as the fellow decided whether to lie about this or not. And saw that he had decided the truth would pay best.

'Inspector, yes. He said he was in shop for last time.'

'And he told you where he was going?'

281

Victor Masters may or may not have done, he thought. Most probably a man who was so careful to conceal where it was he had lived until today would have said nothing. But he might, he just might, have let something slip at a time when, for whatever reason, he was almost certainly putting that shop behind him.

Again, the flicker in the eyes in front of him that spoke of a decision being arrived at.

'Andheri, Inspector. I am helping police to my fullest, yes? He was saying once he would some day go back to Andheri.'

Andheri, Ghote thought. He remembered seeing Masters put his head out of the train coming in to Grant Road when it had reached Andheri Station. At the time he had thought Masters might be getting ready to make a dash for it. But, thinking back, the way he had looked out had not been like that. He had, rather, been giving the scene the sort of long look someone might give a familiar place not visited for some time. So, yes, Andheri: it was very likely.

'To Andheri,' he said. 'Where in Andheri?'

'Inspector, I was not liking to ask. That man is not someone you ask his business. That I am knowing.'

True, Victor Masters, of the hunched shoulders, the hunched face, was not a person you asked unnecessary questions.

'Andheri?' he said. 'Just only that?'

'Yes, Inspector. I swear. I swear. Just only that.'

Ghote tossed the man's knife down a few feet away and turned to go.

A grey-faced Axel Svensson was standing behind him.

'Ganesh. My friend. You wounded him. You drew blood.'

Ghote sadly shook his head. The firinghi had a lot to learn about life in India.

'Axel, a prick only. And the fellow told me something at least. Victor Masters must be somewhere in Andheri. Some luck I have had.'

* * *

Yet as, for the second time, Axel Svensson's taxi brought Ghote just after nightfall to densely packed Andheri, he thought to himself that he had not had any great piece of luck. Yes, almost certainly Victor Masters was somewhere in the area. But it was a big enough area, almost a small town in itself. So how could he track the man down? And with eight hours or more of Mr Kabir's forty-eight already used up.

'Well,' Axel Svensson said, with a cheerfulness Ghote found purely irritating, 'at least this time when we are going to whatever this place is called it isn't raining.'

'Axel, the place is Andheri,' he snapped. 'Andheri. Where I told you the colonies for rail workers are.'

Rail workers, he thought suddenly.

Something else about rail workers and Victor Masters I heard somewh — Yes. Yes, that is it. Yeshwant told us the security guard she bribed said the fellow was always using the twenty-four-hour clock, and must have been in police, army or railways. No trace in army and police records. So can he be ex-Indian Railways? After all, an Anglo-Indian like many . . .

If so — his mind worked rapidly — if so, then it may just be possible he belongs, or has belonged, to that club for retired railmen where, yes, Miss Ivy Cooper was saying her father had long ago been secretary.

It was a chance. It was the barest of chances. But it was at least something to pursue.

'Come along,' he said to the Swede.

'But where, Ganesh? Where to?'

'To be finding, if I can, the railway retirees club. If Victor Masters was ever a member, they may have his address. And he may be at that place.'

A spark of joy, hunter's joy, lit up the Swede's big face.

But before long it was to be extinguished.

They found the club, in the way any address in the city is found, by asking and asking and asking. But when they reached it at last they saw a semi-derelict building. On its paint-flaked green door there was a faded yellowish card with written on it, in ink that had turned a dull shade of purple, just one word: *Closed.*

'But — But what does that mean?' Axel Svensson asked, peering at the word. 'Does it mean this place is closed for today? Or for some holiday? Or — Or for ever?'

'Look at the place, look at it,' Ghote answered, with a sharp note of bitterness. 'Does it damn well look as if it is going to open tomorrow? Or next week? No. No, it is closed for ever. For ever.'

'But can't we . . . Well, can't we — But there must be something we can do.'

Ghote was about to let out a savage reply. But then a thought came to him.

'Yes,' he said. 'Yes, we can go and see Miss Ivy Cooper. We can ask her father if there has ever been in the retirees club one Victor Masters. Or even any other Masters, who might be a relation to our Victor.'

'Yes, but Ganesh . . . '

He left his firinghi friend trailing after him as he made his way rapidly back through the

285

ill-lit streets to the compound where they had seen Ivy Cooper's old father playing his solitary, locked-in patience in the drizzling rain.

But tonight no one was sitting in the broken-backed peacock chair under the dying gul mohar tree. As soon as Ghote saw this, he made straight for the stairs up to Ivy Cooper's flat, with Axel Svensson coming bewilderedly behind.

Miss Ivy Cooper, he thought, will not at all be welcoming the policewalla who was giving her one hard time before. But she must give me her help with her father. Otherwise all I would be able to do is to go here and there about Andheri, perhaps for days, hoping to come upon the man who may hold the key to the Ajmani murder. And Mr Kabir's forty-eight hours will be up long before then.

He knocked at the door of the flat. When Ivy Cooper opened it there wafted out, not the smell of frying but a distinctly unpleasant odour. Nor did she look as much in charge as she had been before. She looked, in fact, as if she was attempting to cope without success with some disaster. Ruby-red spectacles nowhere in evidence, the signs of tears easily to be seen on her desperately plain pock-marked face, sweat patches dark at the underarms of her floral dress.

No, Ghote thought in a swirl of rage against life. The old man is dead. It must be that. Her father. And in that man's head, if anything could have been got out of it, all the names of the members of that retirees club. With among them perhaps the name, and address also, of one Victor Masters. My last hope.

'Madam, Miss Cooper,' he stammered, 'what has happened? It is your father?'

'My father? God knows where the silly old fool is.'

So he is alive. And hope also. But what is then the problem that is making her so upset?

'But, madam, you are in trouble? What it is?'

His questions had scarcely been sympathetic, but evidently Miss Cooper was going to take them as being so.

'Oh, Inspector,' she wailed. 'It's that damn man from the flat below. He's come storming and swearing in here, like some creature from Mars on TV, telling me my drain is choked and the filth is coming into his bathroom. And what am I to do? I know nothing about drains and drainage. Yet there he is, right inside my place, shouting and swearing.'

And no sooner had she said those words than from further inside the flat there came a torrent of abuse, loud as gunfire.

'Miss Copper,' came the voice of the Swede from the balcony, 'perhaps if I was to say a word to that gentleman he would at least stop all that noise.'

No, no, no, Ghote thought.

He foresaw such complications in the clash of cultures ahead — the shouting man was using as much Marathi as English — that he would be kept here far into the night trying to extricate the firinghi, if not having to prevent actual violence.

'Madam,' he said quickly to Ivy Cooper, 'kindly allow myself to deal with your problem.'

She stepped aside, with a promptness that perturbed Ghote. But there was no getting out of it now.

He entered the flat and went through the hall, where not long ago he had broken down the last barriers in Ivy Cooper's mind in his efforts to make her confess to feeding information to Yeshwant. In the dark back quarter of the little flat next to what he took to be the bathroom he made out — the hall tubelight was still intermittently flickering — a small fat man with a dab of a moustache, wearing nothing but the dhoti he had wrapped round his little jutting belly.

'Damn disgrace. Bloody Anglo-Indians. No idea of cleanliness.'

The words were still spouting out.

'Bhai sahib,' Ghote greeted him. 'Try to be calm only. I am sure all this problem can be dealt with.'

The tubby little man whirled round.

'Oh, you are, are you? Then bloody well deal with it. Before I am committing one murder, yes?'

And, pushing past like an escaping black-haired pig, he rushed straight through the hall, where Ivy Cooper was standing gibbering at a perplexed Axel Svensson, and out into the night.

Then Ghote realized that there was nothing for it, if he wanted some collaboration from Pappubhai Chimanlal's usually efficient secretary. He would have to see if he himself could do what her irate neighbour from downstairs had told him to do. *Deal with it.*

Gingerly he opened the flimsy bathroom door. And at once he knew he had found the source of the trouble. The unpleasant smell pervading the flat bounced out at him at double strength.

He put his hand to his nose and clamped tight his nostrils.

Then, in the light of the feeblest of electric bulbs hanging above, he looked more carefully into the cramped space in front of

289

him. There was a tap protruding from the wall, and dripping incessantly. There was a three-legged wooden stool, dirty with long use. There was a red plastic jug resting on the stool. And the low whitish cracks-crazed earthenware pan that occupied the whole floor area was awash to its very top with grey gunge, in which were floating various fragments of vegetables evidently from the dishes that were washed there.

He looked round for some sort of stick with which he could probe about for the choked drain and halt the flow of filthy water that was leaking away though the pan's overflow. There was nothing.

He gritted his teeth, closed his lips tight and rolled up his right shirt-sleeve as far as it would go. Then, squatting down just outside, he plunged his hand into the greasy greyness and felt around. The immediate result was a yet nastier smell rising up.

But eventually, after swishing to and fro in the thick grey liquid — a long brownish piece of tamarind had stuck to his wrist — he located the drain. It was in the furthest corner of the crack-marked pan. Face contorted with disgust, he managed to get his fingernails under the rim of the drain's metal sieve. He pulled it out, slimy with long congealed soap.

With two dull plopping explosions a couple of large bubbles now erupted from the depths of the drain.

For a minute, squatting there, Ghote waited. Perhaps now all the foul liquid would run safely away.

It did not.

He allowed himself to stand up for a moment to ease the strain on his thighs. Then, clamping his mouth yet more firmly shut, he squatted back down and thrust his hand, fingers extended, into the drainpipe. What they reached was the slimy remains of what he at once knew must be a rat.

He could not prevent himself bringing his hand out as if his fingers had encountered a nest of needles. But then he sucked in a breath and went into battle again. It had to be done. If he was to get any sense out of Ivy Cooper, he had to accomplish this task. However foul.

Working his fingers round the soft body, he eventually got enough of a grip on it to be able to try a cautious tug. For a long moment nothing happened. Then at last he felt a slight upward movement. Gently he kept up the hauling pressure. Quarter-inch by quarter-inch the rat's body came up towards him. At last with a sliding rush it slipped totally clear.

At once the stinking grey water in the pan

began running away, forming in a couple of seconds a sluggish whirlpool. Ghote watched it, half-fascinated, the slimy rat still clutched in his fingers. When at last the pan was empty he rose to his feet and dropped the rat into Miss Cooper's red plastic jug.

'Madam,' he called back. 'No problem.'

20

'Where's me dinner?' As Ghote came back from making plentiful use of the bottle of Dettol which Ivy Cooper had provided, he heard the words bawled out from just outside the flat.

The old man, he thought. The old man here just when I am wanting to ask about Victor Masters, possible early retired Indian Railways employee, probable victim of blackmail by the killer of Anil Ajmani. My good deed rewarded.

If I can get answers out of him.

Ivy Cooper had opened the door of the flat.

'Dinner,' she said sharply. 'You'll be lucky if you get even a banana to put down your old throat.'

'What d'you mean? Banana? Aren't I entitled to better than that? What did I bring you up for, you slut, if it wasn't to get me me dinner when I want it?'

At least, Ghote said to himself, the old man is more alert and alive than when I was seeing him last.

'Miss Cooper,' he said, stepping forward,

'there are some questions I would like to ask your father.'

'Questions?' Ivy Cooper snapped. 'You'll be lucky to get even one answer. He's not always as smart as this, you know. Most of the time he's so far away there's never any getting him back.'

'But it is about his far-off days I am wanting to talk. The time when he was, isn't it, Hon. Sec. of railway retirees club?'

'Well, he was that all right. But let me tell you, you won't get a word out of him about those days that makes one anna of sense.'

'But, madam, it is a matter of great importance,' the hulking form of Axel Svensson put in.

'Well, if you say so, sir.'

Ivy Cooper seemed more than a little impressed by this intervention from a white face. She reached for her ruby-red spectacles from the sideboard, put them on and loudly explained to her father that 'the nice gentleman from Home' was going ask him a few questions.

'Mr Cooper,' Ghote said, usurping Axel Svensson's place as soon as they were settled round the stained old table in the middle of the room, 'I am wanting to find one Victor Masters who may once have been a member of your retirees club. Are

294

you recalling that name?'

'No.'

Is the old man just only being obstinate, the way he was before? Or is he truly not recognizing the name *Victor Masters*? And if he is not . . .

But he tried again.

'Mr Cooper, Masters is a good Anglo-Indian name. Are you sure there was no one called that in your club?'

'What you want to know for?'

Ah, this is better. He is just only remembering I am a policewalla, and he is reacting the way he did before. *Bloody police*, he said when he was playing his game of patience down in the compound there and I was stating my rank. So, now get round this one obstacle, and end of tunnel may be in sight.

He gave Ivy Cooper a look pleading for help. And, perhaps thinking of what he had done for her, she came to the rescue.

'Dad, this gentleman's been very kind to us. He unblocked the bathroom drain.'

'Put a rat down it,' the old man said, with a cracked laugh. 'Bleeding pest. But I got him. Caught him with me own hands and shoved the bleeder down there head first. That finished him off, that did.'

Ghote was afraid this would bring his

daughter's fury down on the old man to the exclusion of everything else. But, no, she managed to hold her tongue.

'So, come on, Dad. Fair's fair. Tell the gentlemen what they want to know.'

The old man give her a mutinous look.

'If I can't, I can't.'

'But, Dad, you can. You know the names of every one of those members. You've gone reeling them out to me often enough.'

'Masters,' the old man snapped out. 'Did you ever hear me once say *Masters*?'

'How can I remember when there are so many of them? Come on, Dad, think. Begin from the beginning, if you like. *Alexander, Atkins* . . . That's how it goes, doesn't it?'

'What if it does? It doesn't get to *Masters*. Not ever. I'm telling you that.'

Ivy Cooper looked at Ghote and shrugged.

'I don't think we're going to get anywhere,' she said. 'And he's as spry now as he's been for weeks. For months.'

Ghote let despondency wash over him.

So near, perhaps. And so far. What chance is there now of finding Victor Masters? And in much less than forty-eight hours Mr Kabir will be telling me I am no longer a Crime Branch officer.

Axel Svensson, silent since they had settled round the table, suddenly leaned forward, remembering perhaps his previous role as interpreter to Ghote of Anglo-Indian speech.

'Mr Cooper,' he asked, painfully slowly and precisely. 'Do you recall a certain Victor Masters?'

'Told your mate, I never.'

'But are you sure? A man with a funny twisted jaw and hunched-up shoulders?'

'Oh, him.'

'What? What? You know that man?' Ghote could not contain his excitement.

'Course I do. That's Victor Hinks, I'd know his ugly mug anywhere, twisted jaw an' all. Everybody knows him. The bastard. Sacked from the railway, and then wanted to join the club all the same. We wouldn't have him. Course we wouldn't. I said to him . . . '

He lapsed then into silence and the faraway look came into his eyes, the look Ghote had seen in the dim rainy light of the compound and had all but failed to penetrate. He knew now that they had been only just in time. Old Mr Cooper was back in the retirees club, years ago, fighting an ancient battle. Lost to them.

He turned to Axel Svensson.

'Well done. Well done, Axel,' he said. 'Shabash. We know now that Masters was never that man's name. No wonder he was wanting to hide every fact in his life. He was going under alias. I am not at all able to think yet why he has done that. But it is certain that is what he has been doing. It is accounting for a lot.'

He broke off as he realized Ivy Cooper was sitting there beside her dreaming father, all ears.

'You want to find that fellow?' she asked abruptly.

'You . . . you are knowing him? Knowing where he stays?'

The blood began to run through Ghote's veins as swiftly as a Himalayan torrent.

'Do I know where he lives?' Ivy Cooper gave him an ironic grin. 'I do, and I don't. I know he deserted his wife and kids. Everyone talked about it. And as far as I know he hasn't been seen or heard of from that day to this.'

Yes, Ghote thought. That fits. For some reason, some secret reason, the man has been living in that room in Kamathipura all that time. And for some time past he has been out each night at Shanti Niwas as Victor Masters, the in-charge of the security team.

'But,' he asked Ivy Cooper, 'you are knowing his wife's address?'

'No. No, I don't. I only knew her to talk to when we met in the market, or somewhere like that. She stays somewhere over towards

Jogeshwari Station.'

With that Ghote had to be content.

★   ★   ★

As they went thumping down the wooden stairs to the compound, Ghote had intended to go looking straight away for Victor Masters' wife. But, in the dark at the stairs' foot, he decided, hot on the trail as they were, that he could afford to let pass perhaps another eight of the hours Mr Kabir had allowed him. The trouble hc had got into at the Koli shop in Colaba when, as his old mentor Gross's *Criminal Investigation* used to say, he had been 'an expeditious investigator' was still raw in his mind. And there was, in any case, not much hope of achieving anything till the next day.

So he had taken Axel Svensson back to the Taj, thanked him two or three times for his intervention that had at the last moment produced the true name of Victor Masters, promised him he would take him to Andheri the next day and at last had made his way home.

To find, once more, his wife and son sitting glaring at each other with the TV, evidently once more a bone of contention, switched into silence.

299

He had known he ought to play the peacemaker. But, his head full of his new-made discovery, its implications whirring round to the exclusion of everything else, he just managed to grunt out, 'Tired, going to bed,' and had left them to it.

But next morning, accompanied by his Swedish shadow, he was back bright and early, not in Andheri but in nearby Jogeshwari. And with an idea in his head, the mysteriously arriving product of the thoughts trapped there during the night. Ivy Cooper had mentioned that Victor Masters had left *his wife and kids*. But those kids would, in all probability, go to school, and there was a school near Jogeshwari Station. So it should be possible to find them. Then he should be able discover where precisely they lived. And, with luck and patience, whether their father had reappeared at home as suddenly as he had left his hideout in Kamathipura.

Patience he was in full possession of as they arrived by train at Jogeshwari. Luck, it seemed, was another matter. At the school Ghote's immediate inquiry revealed that the Hinks children, Albert, six, and Gloria, seven, were, yes, pupils there. But both were absent.

'They must be ill,' said the deputy headmistress, solid of face, heavy hornrims, good-quality cotton sari. 'Tomorrow they will bring the mother's letter.'

'Then can you let me have their address?' Ghote asked. 'It is the mother I am wanting to see.'

'It is our policy not to give out addresses.'

Ghote bit his underlip.

'But the children's teacher?' he asked. 'Is one lady teaching both of them? Perhaps I would be able to see her.'

'At this hour she should be in her classroom. You cannot go breaking in there.'

Ghote was on the point of flourishing his identity as a Crime Branch officer, hesitating only because he knew he was still Sam Marlowe rather than Inspector Ghote. But then the deputy headmistress relented.

'However, I remember now Mrs Phanse is also absent. But you may find her at the hostel where she stays. She is in fear of a drunken husband and is often subject to fits of — what shall I say? — of withdrawal. But she is an excellent teacher, and so when she is struck down in that way we send her back to the hostel where she stays. You may be able to see her there.'

The hostel address, apparently, was not a closely guarded secret. Ghote, with Axel Svensson slogging along beside him, reached the place after a ten-minute march through the now crowded, sun-battered streets. The door was standing open and they advanced into the dark hallway beyond. Cautious after his last venture out of the sun and into a dim interior, Ghote hesitated. But in a moment he had made out that no danger faced him. Instead, he saw at the far end of the hallway a peon sitting at a rough wooden table deeply absorbed in some task.

It was only when he had gone forward a step or two more, still peering in the comparative darkness, that he made out what the absorbing task was. The various objects that were the peon's tools of his trade, a paste-pot for doubly sealing envelopes, a tobacco tin holding mixed pins and paper-clips, three fat office pencils, a hank of cotton for wrapping small parcels, an ink-bottle, had been arranged as a sort of obstacle course. And running this course, or rather struggling along it, was a fat brown cockroach trying to reach what looked like a piece of cooked carrot being dangled by the peon from a short length of cotton.

Something about the carrot dangler's faraway absorption kept Ghote, and now Axel Svensson at his elbow, silently watching the man deep in a world of his own. The cockroach blunderingly negotiated the last obstacle but one, the tin of pins and paperclips. And then Ghote saw the peon bring up his other hand from beneath the table, grasping between finger and thumb one of his long office pins. He poised it over the cockroach, savouring the fact that, just as paradise seemed in sight for it, doom was to fall.

'No,' shouted Axel Svensson.

The peon dropped pin and carrot. The cockroach, in utter confusion, scuttled to the table edge and fell off. Ghote stepped smartly forward.

'Police,' he said. 'To see one Mrs Phanse.'

The peon blinked, open-mouthed.

'Mrs Phanse?' he said at last. 'Phanse like *phanse*, the jack-fruit. Yes. Yes, she is here. Room 17, first floor. *Like jack-fruit*, that is what we are always saying.'

Without any further delay, Ghote led Axel Svensson off. All very well for him, god-like, to have saved the cockroach. But cockroaches were pests. Compassion should go only so far.

Room 17. He knocked at its door.

'Come in,' a voice called.

Mrs Phanse, still dressed, it appeared, in the old washed-out sari she wore at night, was sitting on the only chair the bare room possessed, drawn up to its one narrow window.

She scrambled to her feet when she saw the two strangers.

'What — What is it?' she said, her voice rising in panic. 'You are not wanting me? Not from — From him? From my husband? I have left him, you know. Left him for ever.'

'Mrs Phanse,' Ghote replied, as calmly as he could, 'they were giving us your address at the school. I am a police officer. This is Mr Svensson, an observer from Sweden. I have some questions I wish to ask you, nothing to do with any husband whatsoever.'

'No, madam, no, certainly not,' Axel Svensson put in with lumbering eagerness.

'Yes? Then what is it? What do you want to ask me? I am safe here. Safe. In the hostel. This is a women's area. You should not be coming pushing in.'

'Madam,' Ghote said, 'we are here in pursuance of duty. It is quite right for us to come. All we are doing is trying and attempting to find one Mrs Hinks, the mother of Albert and Gloria in your class at the school.'

Then, even as he said the words, something stirred in his mind. *Hinks. Hinks.* He had heard someone speak about a Hinks, and before Axel Svensson had brought to light the fact that Victor Masters was Victor Hinks. Only, it had not been a Victor —

Yes. Yes, this is it. Adik, in praising his own first-class work out at Shanti Niwas, had said

Anil Ajmani's PA before the present one had been killed in some brawl six years ago. And his name was Vincent Hinks. So . . . so can that man be Victor Hinks's brother? Victor and Vincent, it was perfectly likely. And if so . . .

Abruptly he changed his line of questioning.

'Madam, are you knowing anything of the Hinks family? The father is one Victor Hinks, yes? Madam, did he once have a brother going by the name of Vincent, Vincent Hinks?'

And, to his total surprise, a deep blush came up on Mrs Phanse's strained face.

'Vincent,' she murmured, 'my poor Vincent.'

She looked straight at Ghote.

'Once I was in love with Vincent Hinks,' she said. 'Before — Before I was married to — To that nasty drunk. In love, yes. He was so handsome, so fair and so clever too. He could do anything. No wonder everybody loved and admired him. Even his ugly brother. But he — He was in love with that rich girl where he was personal assistant. It was going to be a love-match. Then — You are knowing Vincent was killed, yes?'

'Yes. Yes, madam, I am knowing such. It was in some fight.'

'Oh, no, Inspector, it was not.'

'Not?'

'No. No, Vincent was murdered. And I can tell you who was murdering him, if not with his own hands, with the aid of a hired supari using some horrible knife, like a fish knife. It was his boss. His boss, Mr Anil Ajmani, Ajmani Air-Conditioning.'

'Madam,' Ghote said hurriedly, the thoughts in his head darting and linking and twisting round too fast to capture. 'I see you are very much in distress. We will take leave now. And thank you.'

When he had ushered out a bewildered Axel Svensson, he took him by the arm and marched him three or four yards down the corridor.

'Axel,' he said, 'I have something to tell. I am knowing now why Victor Hinks was taking alias as Victor Masters. The murderer of Anil Ajmani is not the man who was blackmailing Victor Masters to keep locked up the dogs at Shanti Niwas. No, the murderer is no one else but Victor Hinks, alias Victor Masters, himself.'

21

'Mr Kabir, sir,' Inspector Ghote said. 'There is a matter I have to inform you.'

Yes, he thought, in a flash of instant reevaluation. Yes, now I have done it. I am about to tell Mr Kabir that everything his top team was working at over at Shanti Niwas, that protected-protected zone of safety Anil Ajmani was building round himself, was just only one bloody waste of time. And will he believe me? Have I done enough to make certain he will? Am I right even?

'You're going to tell me you've laid that damn Yeshwant by the heels at last, Inspector?'

'No, sir, no. Sir, it is the Ajmani case.'

'Ajmani? That's got nothing to do with you, Inspector. Do you mean to tell me you have been poking your nose in at Shanti Niwas instead of obeying my direct orders?'

'Sir, yes. But, sir — Sir, it was by chance only, in course of Yeshwant inquiries, sir, that I was learning what I have.'

'Inspector, it had better be something good and hard, or you'll be finding yourself

clearing your desk before another hour's gone
by.'

'Yes, sir. I think it is good, sir, and hard
also. Sir, I am able to name the murderer of
Mr Anil Ajmani.'

There. Said. And now the task of proving
it. And quickly. Or I will be finding, yes,
myself clearing my desk, as he is saying.
Perhaps also getting no other desk to be
seated at.

'Inspector — '

'Sir, it is Mr Victor Masters, security
in-charge at Shanti Niwas.'

'Oh, it is, is it, Inspector? So why do you
think Mr Adik, who has been up at the house
every day since the murder took place, has
not told me this fellow committed the crime?'

Oh, it is all coming true. Just as I was
forecasting and fearing. He is setting his mind
one hundred per cent against whatsoever I
may say.

'Sir, it is this. Inspector Adik was not
knowing what I have just only this morning at
last found out.'

'Oh, he wasn't, wasn't he? So, what is this
piece of vital information you've got it into
your head that you know and no one else
does? Spit it out, man. Spit it out. If you can.'

Now, do it. Say it. Yes, spit same out. But
spit all in one good piece. Or . . .

'Yes, sir. Sir, it is that the said Victor Masters is not at all such. Sir, he is one Victor Hinks. And, sir, he was once having a brother, Vincent Hinks by name, who, sir, six years ago was murdered. Victim of supari killing.'

And not finished yet. Hardest part of all perhaps yet to come. Do it, say it. And wait for one damn explosion.

'Sir, that killing was paid for by Shri Anil Ajmani himself.'

But Deputy Commissioner Kabir stayed silent.

Is he remembering and recalling facts about Mr Anil Ajmani, businessman who was building up air-conditioner empire by altogether ruthless means? Are facts, conveniently hidden but there to those who know, about union organizers who were killed in mysterious circumstances coming back into his mind? And other nefarious deeds also?

Time passed. Leaden time. A whole minute. More.

Then the Deputy Commissioner spoke again, sounding now somehow less fiercely British.

'Inspector, you are sure of this? You're sure of your facts? Sure beyond doubt?'

Am I? Yes, I was, or I was thinking I was. When I was facing prospect of Mr Kabir's anger. But now it is different. He has taken in

309

what I have said. He has remembered what he has. He has thought about same. And he is ready to believe, and to act on what I have said. But he is feeling he must be sure, doubly sure. And now, suddenly, I am asking myself if I have got it right. Or if in the end, somehow, I have got it all wrong.

But, no. No, no, no. I am right. I must be. This is the truth of what was happening that night at Shanti Niwas. It is.

'Sir, yes. Yes, sir, I am one hundred per cent certain of circumstances. Sir, I was hearing this-all from the teacher of Victor Hinks's children. She is well knowing whole family, sir, and some years past also she was believing Vincent Hinks was going to marry her. Sir, a first-class witness.'

Or is she?

Abruptly another streak of doubt shot like a lightning flash through Ghote's mind.

Mrs Phanse — *phanse* like the jack-fruit — wasn't she after all a woman who had to take leave from her school because of her troubled mind? Hadn't he found her in that room at her hostel sitting lost to the real world around her? Locked in the only thoughts she could bear to think?

'A first-class witness? Is she indeed? Well, we won't go into why you were talking to her, not at the present moment. What I think we'd

310

better do, if he's still in the building, is to have Inspector Adik up.'

He reached for his internal telephone, barked out an inquiry, put the handset down.

'He's on his way.'

For several long minutes silence hung in the air in the big cabin, with its enormous wall-map of Bombay, its large, painted, pin-dotted board detailing the whereabouts of every single officer in Crime Branch. Only the whirring of the tall standing fan that kept Mr Kabir cool made itself evident.

Ghote stood there, at attention, forcing himself to keep his mind blank of all thought.

At last there came a brisk tap on the door and Adik entered, marched across to the desk, clicked heels.

'Sir?'

'Adik, Inspector Ghote here has just told me a certain fact, at least I hope for his sake it is a fact, which may materially alter the Ajmani investigation.'

'Yes, sir?'

'Tell him, Ghote.'

A gulp.

'It is this, Adik bh — It is this, Inspector. I have been able to discover that the Shanti Niwas head of security is not at all one Victor Masters. That is, he is such, but he is going under false name. He is really Victor Hinks, brother of one Vincent Hinks who was, as you yourself were mentioning, Mr Anil Ajmani's former PA. Killed in a brawl also you were saying. And I have found out that Ajmani sahib had good reasons for wanting end to life of said Vincent Hinks.'

'This is true, Ghote?'

'He tells me it is,' Mr Kabir put in.

'Then, DCP, this may be important.'

'And, sir,' Ghote broke in, feeling how he was being listened to with full attention both by Adik and Mr Kabir, 'who only but the head of security at Shanti Niwas could have entered that house without causing those dogs, always prowling outside during hours of darkness, to make one barking hullabaloo?'

'The dogs in the night-time,' Mr Kabir said thoughtfully. 'So, Ghote, you're something of a Sherlock Holmes, eh?'

Ghote was baffled. Why should Mr Kabir suddenly call him as a Holmes? But much that Mr Kabir said had always baffled him.

'No, sir, no,' he ploughed on. 'It is just that I was finding out certain things, and I was able to put together two, sir, and two.'

'I don't suppose Holmes ever claimed to be able to do much more than that, once he had obtained his data. So what else did your simple sum tell you, Inspector?'

'Well, sir, I was happening to learn also that Mr Ajmani's daughter, one of the Yeshwant victims I was interviewing, sir, now Mrs Latika Patel, wife of Mr R. K. Patel, MLA, was six-seven years ago contemplating one love-match. And, sir, it was with the altogether tall, handsome, clever and fair Vincent Hinks.'

'Wait a minute,' Inspector Adik broke in. 'You have got the wrong man. I've never seen Vincent Hinks, after all killed some six-seven years past. But no one could say he can have been fair and handsome, however clever he may have been to rise up to be Anil Ajmani's PA. Just look at the man you say is his brother. Victor Masters is as ugly a devil as you could wish to see. The two cannot be sons of same father.'

Ghote felt an abrupt downward plunge of deflation. Is Adik right? And, if so, was Mrs Phanse altogether wrong after all?

But deflation lasted for no more than two seconds.

'No,' he exclaimed. 'No, Adik, brothers do not have to look so much of alike. I have a Swedish friend, here in the city at this moment, a very tall and upstanding man. And he was telling he has a brother who is short almost to dwarf.'

'Well, yes,' Mr Kabir put in. 'Brothers can

look very different. Why, in my own family . . . '

He let the ramifications of his distinguished brahmin clan fade into anonymity.

'So, you see,' Ghote began again, once more inwardly triumphant, 'Victor Hinks is having one strong motive for killing Mr Ajmani. He was believing that six-seven years ago Ajmani sahib, when he found his daughter was proposing to marry an Anglo-Indian from nowhere itself, gave instructions, and some goonda one night was knifing to death this Vincent Hinks. Sir, I believe it was with a fish knife.'

'Like the one I myself found in the fountain at Shanti Niwas,' Adik came in, staking a claim.

'And like one I have seen in a Koli shop in Colaba where Victor Masters was a customer', Ghote added, seeing once again the shop-owner snatching from the wall a long fish knife and coming threateningly towards him.

'Good man,' Mr Kabir murmured.

'And, yes,' Ghote resumed, feeling now his two listeners were all ears. 'Yes, Victor Hinks was worshipping his more clever and fair brother. I was told this with full details by Mrs Phanse. So when Victor came to believe his much worshipped brother had been killed at behest only of late Anil Ajmani in order to stop the marriage — Miss Latika was soon after married off to R. K. Patel, very big dowry, I expect — he was making up his mind and determining to take revenge. So he was disappearing from wife and family and taking new name, because he was not at all willing to pay for crime he was intending to commit. He was finding a room to stay at. It is in Kamathipura. I have seen it. And then he was finding job as security guard. He was working his way up, until not long ago he was becoming in-charge at Shanti Niwas. Then, now inside ring of security at that House of Peace, he soon saw how he would be able to reach Anil Ajmani in his den itself, with no one knowing how a murderer could have got through all the securities there.'

For a long moment silence again pervaded the big cabin. Then Mr Kabir spoke.

'This room in Kamathipura, is the fellow still there?'

'No, sir. Yesterday he was leaving same. He must be thinking he has got away with his murder and can go back to being one Victor Hinks, father of a family in Jogeshwari.'

'So we'll find him at Jogeshwari,' Mr Kabir said, half rising from his seat.

'No, sir,' Inspector Adik put in, 'I think you'll actually find him up at Shanti Niwas. I understand he is there today, being paid off since high-level security is no longer needed.'

'All right.' Mr Kabir swung round from his desk. 'Let's go, Adik. You've got transport?'

'Sir.'

But then, as he left, Mr Kabir turned for a moment to Ghote.

'Yes, Inspector,' he said. 'Yes, report to me tomorrow, will you? There's a rather tricky case that's just come up to me. I think you're the chap to handle it.'

Ghote stood by the big desk, watching the cabin door swing to and fro in the wake of the Deputy Commissioner and a hurrying Inspector Adik.

Soon his head became filled with pleasantly vague thoughts.

THE END

We do hope that you have enjoyed reading this large print book.

Did you know that all of our titles are available for purchase?

We publish a wide range of high quality large print books including:
Romances, Mysteries, Classics
General Fiction
Non Fiction and Westerns

Special interest titles available in large print are:
The Little Oxford Dictionary
Music Book
Song Book
Hymn Book
Service Book

Also available from us courtesy of Oxford University Press:
Young Readers' Dictionary
(large print edition)
Young Readers' Thesaurus
(large print edition)

For further information or a free brochure, please contact us at:
Ulverscroft Large Print Books Ltd.,
The Green, Bradgate Road, Anstey,
Leicester, LE7 7FU, England.
Tel: (00 44) 0116 236 4325
Fax: (00 44) 0116 234 0205

Other titles in the
Ulverscroft Large Print Series:

MERMAID'S GROUND

Alice Marlow

It's been five years since Kate Williams' beloved husband died, leaving her with two young children to raise. Now she's built a good life in one of Wiltshire's prettiest villages, and she has her dream job, as gardener at Moxham Court. For the last year, Kate has had a lover, roguishly attractive Justin Spencer, but he won't commit to more than a night here and there. When she takes in a male lodger, Jem, Kate's secretly hoping his presence will provoke a jealous reaction in Justin. What she hasn't reckoned on is exactly how attractive Jem will turn out to be.

HOT POPPIES

Reggie Nadelson

A murder in New York's diamond district. A dead Chinese girl with a photograph in her pocket. A plastic bag of irradiated heroin in an empty apartment. A fire in a Chinatown sweatshop. The worst blizzard in New York's history. These events conspire to bring ex-cop Artie Cohen out of retirement and back into the obsessive world of murder and politics that nearly killed him. The terrifying plot uncoils first in New York — in Artie's own back yard — then in Hong Kong, where everything — and everyone — is for sale.

SUMMER OF SECRETS

Grace Thompson

When Bettrys Hopkyns' alcoholic sister Eirlys committed suicide, Bettrys was determined that Eirlys's baby daughter Cheryl — the result of Eirlys's secretive summer love affair — would stay with her. Still yearning for Brett, her former lover, Bettrys sets herself a challenge: to find Cheryl's father. Her search takes her and Cheryl to a small seaside village in west Wales; to a close-knit community seething with secrets. Befriended by the cheerful Gordon, who falls in love with her, Bettrys is quickly drawn into a web of deceit and is forced to face the terrifying possibility that Brett might be a murderer . . .

A MORTAL AFFAIR

Stella Allan

Frances Parry seemed to have it made. She was married to a Harley Street consultant, she had a beautiful home, wealthy friends — including the fascinating Bernard, her husband's friend since undergraduate days — and a creative job. But suddenly Frances's world was turned upside down; her home was sold, her sideline job became a vital means of livelihood, and Bernard, who had become her lover, was exposed as a criminal. And then Frances found that she herself was indulging in criminal activities in a deadly duel with the law.

PROUD HEART, FAIR LADY

Elayn Duffy

Viscount Philip Devlin is not a happy man. From his grave, his father has decreed that the Viscount shall marry a girl he has never met if he is to inherit his beloved Meadowsdene and Kingsgrey Court. For a girl with no dowry to speak of, marrying into one of the oldest, richest houses in England is good fortune indeed. But the Viscount's bride, Kathryn Hastings, faces a grim future for she will be his wife in name only, leaving him to pursue his life as before. Kathryn decides to enact her revenge and turns the tables on Devlin.